Karina

a novel

TONYE PORBENI ADENUSI

EFFIE GRACE

KARINA

First published by in 2020 by Effie Grace

All characters and events in this publication, other than those clearly in the public domain, are fictitious and any resemblance to real persons, living or dead, is purely coincidental.

ISBN: 978-1-5272-8117-2

Cover design: Box of Matches

For my Father, who helped me see that I was enough.
For my feisty Mama, who showed me that love is all.
For my Family, because you make me complete.

PART ONE

CHAPTER ONE

Karina, 2017

The sound of a runaway train reaches my ears before I feel it in my chest. My heart threatening to escape its cage. My eyes snap open, but I see nothing in the engulfing darkness. The bedcovers are in a mess by my feet, which seem poised to run from the faceless pursuer in my dreams. Almost like a film on a loop, this is my constant dream.

What makes us relive dreams over and over, reacting the same way each time – breathless, heart thudding, sweating, sometimes forgetting the exact events that caused our fear?

This one differed slightly from the others. More real. Intense. My mouth opens, but my voice fails me as I try, and fail, to scream. My head feels heavy, and though I reach for the bedside lamp, my limbs – replaced with lead – simply will not move. I remind myself to breathe and watch as the edges of my dream disappear.

The white walls of my bedroom and familiar yellow and grey furnishings slowly come into focus and remind me where I am. Somewhere safe. I lift my arm to check the time. The dim glow from my Apple Watch reads 01:57. Taking a deep breath, I repeat the words I've heard my mother say a thousand times before. 'It was a dream, Karina. It was just a dream,' until my racing heart slows, and my mind relaxes back into sleep.

Two-and-a-half hours pass, and my mind jolts me awake again. Unable to go back to sleep this time, I plod to the kitchen to make myself a cup of chamomile tea, before snuggling in the overstuffed armchair in the corner of my bedroom. 'I'm marrying Tosan James today,' I whisper to myself.

I should be excited, but I feel nothing. I try again, testing the name on my lips, 'Karina James. Mrs Karina James. Mrs James.' I wonder aloud if I should keep my maiden name instead. Karina Thompson sounds better than Karina James. Familiar.

The house is quiet, but I know it won't remain that way for much longer. By six-thirty, the house will be bustling with people putting finishing touches to what has been months of preparation for my wedding. In the corner of my bedroom, my bridal bouquet sits in a small bucket of water to keep it fresh: a cream profusion of calla lilies, trailing pale yellow and pink roses of every size, baby's breath fern, and studded with diamante. My mum has outdone herself. Soon, she will be fussing with the bridesmaids' flowers, which will undoubtedly reflect mine.

My mum's attention to detail may be legendary, but those posies will not be slowing her down from simultaneously issuing instructions for the magnificent centrepieces. The other arrangements will be left in Mrs. Uche's capable hands.

The hairdresser will arrive at an inconveniently early time to fix my hair, and probably pout again when I refuse to have the Brazilian hair weave she so insists is better than my cropped, curly hair.

In the coming hours, chaos will reign supreme. Though I'm feeling less than enthusiastic about it all, I try to enjoy this moment to savour the peace and quiet. Sitting in my favourite "thinking chair" - as Mum calls it - usually calms me. Today, though, something is off. The combination doesn't have its usual calming effect on me, so I decide that if stillness won't bring me peace, then perhaps action might. A run might help me burn away some of that nervous energy.

The trusty alarm clock across the room faithfully shines 05:43. There's still time to get out before the house is fully awake, and I take advantage of the time. If Mum sees me heading out, she'll try to stop me, so I get moving. I jam a pale blue t-shirt over my head, jump into black running shorts, and shove my feet into my well-worn Nike trainers. My feet creep down the hall and out the front door, hoping to escape undetected.

There is a large field with a running track, right in the centre of the plush housing estate where we live in Ikoyi, Lagos. Our haven in the bustling metropolis that is Africa's most populous city, its houses even look like snobs with their ornate gates, manicured gardens and profusion of flowers. My legs carry me towards the track from memory. I don't have to think about where I'm going. With the frustration of my restless night, I hit the track hard, speeding my pace after a brief warm up. I am determined to run off my angst. Despite the early hour, a few regular runners are there, and we nod to one another. No time for talking.

Twenty minutes later, a powerfully built runner catches up to me. It's my friend Akin. He joins me without speaking and, apart from a grunt of acknowledgement, we run a few more laps of the field in silence. My smooth skin glistens with sweat as my body powers through the punishing pace. I run until my legs can take no more and my muscles scream for mercy. They give out on a grassy knoll beside the track. Akin powers through the rest of his run while I settle my breathing and close my eyes to relax.

'Hey you,' he pants, trying to catch his breath.

'Hey back,' I respond without opening my eyes. My hands are resting by my head and my fingers fidget with the slim gold bracelet that's always wrapped around my right wrist. A gift from my parents.

Akin pulls out a bottle of cold water from his bag and takes a long, satisfying drink from it, smacks his lips and says 'ahhh.'

I hate it when people do that, and Akin knows this. The loud gulping sound as the water makes its way down their throat, followed by the lip-smacking and silent 'ahhhh,' as they examine the bottle as if it holds the secret to eternal youth. So irritating. I'm pretty sure this is a purely masculine habit.

My usual quip about his drinking habit does not escape my lips today. Akin looks quizzically at me and sits down beside me to watch the other runners for a minute or five.

'Happy birthday,' spoken with a gentle nudge. 'I know it's not until tomorrow, but you'll be off honeymooning, so... Well, here you go.' He reaches into his bag and pulls out a small, gift-wrapped box. He gives it to me with a wink.

'Oh Akin! Thank you.' My smile widens as my hands accept the gift. As usual, I'd forgotten about my birthday. Akin never forgets.

My fingers tear at the pink and white paper to find a pair of asymmetrical, matte black earrings nestled in the box. I gasp as I recognise the magnificent earrings I'd been admiring a few weeks ago when we shopped for a new phone for Akin. Their simple, yet bold design appealed to my quirky sense of fashion. This time I smile ear-to-ear, grateful for the thoughtful gesture.

'You like?' he's like a child sometimes, so eager to please.

'I love them, Akin, thanks.' I place them back in the box and set it to one side.

Akin shakes his head at me. 'I don't know any other girl who forgets her birthday, apart from you.'

I stick my tongue out at him, and he laughs. 'And as for your less than exuberant response, what's a guy got to do to get some love around here? Your boy should be rewarded for at least remembering your birthday!'

'Dude, please! Who wants to be reminded of getting older? So, no hugs because you're sweaty and smelly, but,' planting a kiss on his cheek, 'thank you for my lovely earrings.'

Akin snorts. 'Right. So, you call yourself an old woman at age 30? Wait until you're my age! Anyway, I'm glad you like the earrings.'

'You're only eighteen months older than me, Akin,' I laugh.

As the moment settles, my smile fades and I stare across the track. My mind has drifted off on the breeze. Akin's finger whispers a touch on the back of my hand and draws my mind back to him.

'What's up? You're getting married in a few hours. I thought you would be at least pretending to primp and preen. Instead, I find you here, running like you are hoping to fly away. Talk to me, girl. What's on your mind?'

'Akin, please leave me alone,' I attempt to brush him off, waving my hand as if to swat a fly, but it is half-hearted at best. 'I just needed to get out of the house. The day hasn't yet begun and I feel overwhelmed. Why we must have this big wedding, I don't know! So much fussing.' I hold up my hand to tick off fingers, 'The cake, the hair, the flowers, the guest list, the food... The list never ends and I'm just so tired of it all.' With a growl, I duck my head and furrow my eyebrows.

Silence follows my outburst as Akin gives me time to calm down. After a few minutes, I look up to find him watching me closely. Blinking quickly, I'm a little surprised by the tears that are threatening to fall. Any more kindness from him could make me more emotional than I care for right now.

'Why are you looking at me like that?' I ask, feeling more than a little self-conscious. Akin sees right through my bravado and for a moment, we're locked in a silent battle of wills as I dare him with my eyes to discuss the proverbial elephant in the room, or the field in this case.

A sigh of relief escapes from me when he backs down and turns on a cheeky smile. 'Well, Karina, I have asked you to run away with me several times...' He resurrects his pseudo-American drawl to ease the tension. Despite my resistance, laughter gets the best of both of us.

'Akin, you're such an idiot! One of these days you'll get in trouble with Tosan for flirting with me like this. Stop it, *jor*!' I swat ineffectually at his arm playfully, defaulting to coloquiaism for 'please'.

'That's Dr Idiot or Dr Flirt to you, young lady,' his mock outrage makes me chuckle.

Akin and I met through Tosan during our first year at University, and we have been firm friends ever since. Akin is Tosan's buddy and best man at our wedding today. And despite his claims of undying love for me and offers to elope, he has a girlfriend.

She's nice enough.

We chat about inane things for a while, and I am surprised when he stands up and starts to pull me to my feet. 'Come on, you. I've got to deliver you home before your mum sends out a search party. And

I would hate to be the one to tell Tosan that the reason you showed up with your hair undone was because we forgot ourselves again. Together.'

It's a running joke that Akin and I can get lost anywhere if we were together because we always have stuff to talk about. I'm not sure Tosan finds it all that funny though. His laugh appears to be more strained each time someone brings it up.

Something about Akin mentioning my hair irritates me. Tosan and I have discussed my hair several times - he likes weaves and wigs, I prefer the natural look - but it would seem that my look is not complete until I look the part – complete with the Brazilian hair.

I resist the tug on my arm, busying myself with dusting off my clothes and picking bits of grass off my shorts and legs. 'Actually, I don't think I'm ready to go home yet. Why don't you leave me here? I'll head home in about fifteen minutes.'

He argues, reluctant to leave me by myself, 'Now what kind of friend would I be if I listened to that kind of talk? Honey, I know something's up with you and I wish you would tell me.' His brows furrow in concern and I feel bad for doing this, but I need some space. I manage a sigh. My throat is closed tight, and I don't speak for a moment.

'I'll be fine. I'm a tad overwhelmed, but I'll be fine. You go on. Let me sit here with my thoughts for a bit and then I'll go home.' I wave him off, 'I'll see you later.'

He gives up, but his face betrays his inner struggle – should he insist on drawing me out or walk away? I'm relieved as I see his instinct give way to my request for space. Before he walks away, he says, 'Seriously though, Karina, you know where I am if you want to talk.' With a quick hug, he picks up his bag and leaves me sitting on the mound, completely alone with my thoughts.

The sun hides behind a cloud and a cool, gentle breeze blows on my neck as I pluck away at a bit of grass by my feet, making a bald patch even balder. I feel myself being pulled away, sucked into a vortex of memories that I would rather do without today. Playing barefoot in the sand; the mango tree in my parent's front yard; standing outside savouring that musty, earthy smell as the first raindrops come down. Hiding in the uncompleted annex next door, playing hide and seek, and then the cloying smell of onions and a musty body odour. My eyes squeeze tight and my head rattles from side to side, trying to escape memories which are impossible to run from.

CHAPTER TWO

Karina, 1997

Laughter rang out from the pool house as servers carrying trays of food passed between tables. On the loudspeaker, Mighty Sparrow was singing about Jean and Dinah.

'Aha!' my brother, Daniel, was triumphant. 'Didn't I tell you that Mighty Sparrow would be on when we got here?'

Kaine and I rolled our eyes, unimpressed.

'He did say that Karina, which means you have to give him your sweets today.' As the youngest of the family, Preye was often caught between me and Dan.

I turned to my cousin Kaine to say, 'Thank God I don't have any sweets then,' but she was no longer paying attention. Her eyes were on a cute boy who had just walked by.

It was Saturday, and as usual we had come with Dad to Port Harcourt Club. We arrived at the club around ten o'clock and swam while Dad played tennis with his friends. This was our Saturday routine. The clubhouse was like an old friend. The sweet aroma of roasted meats and pastries mingled with the faint smell of the pool, cigarettes and adult drinks to create a unique smell that was comforting. People always seemed to enjoy themselves here - children shrieked and adults talked in at the top of their voices.

Today, Mum had come with us, which was rare, but today was special. I liked that whenever she came, she got in the pool with us and didn't mind getting her hair wet. Not like the other mothers. They preferred to sit in the clubhouse chatting, while their nannies stood gathered by the poolside and gossiped while watching their charges cavort in the pool.

'Mum!' Preye called to get Mum's attention. 'Mum, look at me!' Preye was standing at the side of the pool in her red and white Minnie Mouse costume, which used to be mine. She was about to jump in.

'Oh, Preye wait a minute. You might hurt yourself. Wait for me to get closer, then you can jump to me.' She didn't know that Preye did this ever week - launching herself into the pool with her knees pulled up to her chest, so she could make a water bomb.

While we did our best to get out of the way, Mum wrestled the water to get to Preye, which made us laugh. Kaine, Daniel and I knew what was coming.

When we tired of splashing each other in the pool and diving in at the deep end, we dried ourselves off and went to the clubhouse for something to eat.

Mum's braids had been piled atop her head, but the ends were wet and dripped water down her back. A group of men stopped talking as she walked by and looked at her bottom instead. Maybe they liked her towel. We made our way to bar and mum busied herself, looking in her large, woven bag. Kaine and Daniel were arguing about something as mum pulled out her wallet. 'Right, you two stop arguing. I'm going to get us some snacks and then we're off. So, what would you like to eat?'

'Ah madam, don't worry,' the man at the bar knew us on sight. 'I know what they will eat.' He pointed at us one after the other, furrowing his forehead and calling out our usual orders as he went, 'Club sandwich and a coke, one shawarma and one meatpie with a bottle Fanta. Am I right?'

'Yes please,' Daniel replied for all us as his stomach rumbled and we laughed.

'Would you like to choose a table, and someone will bring over your food?'

'Yes please!' Swimming always gave us an appetite.

'Actually, no thank you,' Mum was rooting through her bag and didn't look up at us. She found her wallet, counted out some notes and handed them to the man. 'Sorry but please ignore them. We'll take a mixture of sausage rolls, meat pies and cans of Coke. Please add some chicken *suya* as well and wrap it all up to take away.'

'Yes ma.' He shot us a quick wink before leaving to get our food.

Mum, seeing our disappointed faces, carried on, 'guys, don't forget we're taking Karina to school today after lunch. We must leave soon so she can get ready.'

She took no notice of our grumbling, telling us to go and 'change out of those wet things' instead. It was a treat to have her with us on a Saturday, so it didn't matter that she didn't know what we like to eat at the club. She worked most Saturdays at Atlantic Maternity Hospital as a doctor. She said her job was a miracle because she got to bring children into the world.

As we hastened to the changing room, Preye slipped her little hand in mine 'Why again are you going to boarding school, Karina?' She couldn't understand why I was going when Dan and she were staying at home.

'I just want to see what it's like, Preye. It will be fun. Like a sleepover.' I would miss her, but I was excited to be going to school. Mum and I had spent the last few weeks buying provisions from the school list and getting my new uniforms ready. I now had a charcoal iron for ironing my uniforms, but I didn't know how to use it, and I was sure I would stain my white blouses with charcoal.

I was in Form One and had been going to school as a day student, but one day in the second term I announced to my parents that I wanted to be a boarder. It meant that I would leave the highly regarded Federal Government College where Dan and I went for a lesser regarded State school. Mum and Dad did their best to dissuade me, but I was adamant. I wanted to be a boarder. When they said no, I became disruptive in school and at home. I pouted and begged Dad because I knew he would listen to me. I told him how some kids had teased me for being fat and had pushed me into a locker so I couldn't breathe. I didn't remember who they were, I said, there were too many of them. It wasn't true, but he didn't know that. Mum always said I should stand up to bullies, and if they called me fat then I should tell them to get lost. It was baby fat, she said, but perhaps I should try not to eat so much. I lied until Dad gave in. Then I left him to convince my mum. Eventually, they gave in and sent me to Livingstone School. I was joining in the third term, but I didn't mind.

When we emerged from the changing rooms, Mum and Dad were waiting for us.

Port Harcourt is called the Garden City of Nigeria. I knew this because the radio jingles said so all the time, 'help to keep Port Harcourt clean… the Garden City of Nigeria.' But driving through D/Line on our way home, I thought I could forgive anyone for thinking this was the Rubbish City of Nigeria - flowers and rubbish jostled for space on the roundabouts and near the vegetable market. I wondered if the people who named the city had eyes in their heads.

We dropped Kaine at her house before going home. I hugged her and my aunt Emi, knowing that I'd miss Kaine terribly. She was more like my sister than a cousin. We promised to write each other often.

After we had lunch, I changed into my yellow and white gingham House dress. Then before I knew it, piling into the car and waving goodbye to the maids and heading off to school. Dan, Preye and I chatted away as we rode in the back of the car, and it wasn't long before we pulled up to the school gates.

"*Livingstone Girls' Secondary School*" an imposing signboard announced our destination, and we pressed our noses against the windows to take in the tall trees lining the short road leading from the gate and to the school buildings. Older students who were returning to school hailed one another, smiling and hugging friends as though they had been away for a year, rather than the usual three to four weeks of Christmas holiday. Mixed with these were a few small, eager faces, looking about with eyes like saucers as they took in their surroundings. I caught the eye of one girl and offered a tentative smile. The smile she returned was brief and shy. I wondered if her tummy, like mine, felt as if she needed the toilet. And if she, too, was already missing her family even though we had just arrived at school.

'Excuse me please,' Dad wound down his window to speak to a man in a yellow tabard, with a clipboard in his hand.

'Yes sir, how can I help you?'

'Please can you tell us where Primrose House is?' Dormitories were assigned based on school houses.

'What is your daughter's name, sir?'

''Karina Thompson,' he replied.

The man muttered to himself as he looked for my name and I knew he wouldn't find it on his clipboard, because Mum always used my full name for important things - *Ayebakarinateh.*

When he finally found me on his list he said, 'Okay, Sir. Primrose House is in that quadrangle on your right, so if you park your car by the building, your wife and son can help her take her things into the dormitory. Please don't enter with them sir, we do not allow men in the hostels.'

'Yes, yes, thank you,' Dad was already easing the car away towards the direction the man had pointed. At the side of the road, families gathered around open car boots and doors, lifting things out. Students in different coloured check dresses were carrying cases, buckets, hoes, and brooms from their cars and disappearing into the dorms. The air pulsed with a life of its own, wrapping all who emerged in busyness and anticipation. As one family finished their goodbyes and pulled away, Dad slipped our car into the vacant spot.

'Okay baby girl, we're here now. Everybody out of the car! Let's see Karina's new house.' Dad unfolded his tall frame out of the car and got my things from the boot. Dan and I did the carrying, naturally.

My "new house" as he called it was a long open room, with rows of beds on either side. 'Where are the bedrooms, Mum?' I tugged at her handbag, feeling suddenly rather small. She took my hand and led me to a small spring bed with no mattress - Daniel would bring my mattress in from the car. A piece of paper with my name printed across the middle sat on the locker next to it.

'There are no bedrooms, baby girl. This is your dorm, and you will sleep here with all the other girls.'

'But where will we dress?' I looked around, hoping for privacy. There was none. Some curtains to draw around my bed would be nice, I thought. I didn't want anybody to see me dress. I shuddered at the thought of being watched by so many people, then gave myself a mental shake, 'Stop it Karina. You will be fine.'

Mum drew me close briefly, 'Don't worry my darling, you will be fine. You'll get used to it. Besides, I found a nice girl to be your school mother. Her name is Juliet Okoro. She's your house prefect.' We looked around us as though expecting Juliet to materialise out of thin air. She didn't.

'Karina?' Daniel had brought my mattress in from the car, 'Go and bring your other things now, Dad says we should hurry up.'

I did as I was told. By the time I got settled and unpacked, it was time for them to leave. Preye helped me put my provisions away in my locker and I placed my metal bucket under my bed like I saw others doing, wondering how on earth we were meant to carry them when they were filled with water. Coming to boarding school didn't seem like such a great idea after all. Mum watched me dress my bed like she had shown me at home. As more girls came in with their families and got settled, she talked with other mothers and told us to behave ourselves.

When she was satisfied, she looked around 'Okay girl, time for us to leave. Where is Juliet?'

We didn't see her, so Mum told me to introduce myself when she arrived. Then we walked to the car and I hugged everybody and tried not to cry when Dad looked sad and Preye said 'Karina, won't you come home with us?' I remembered the girl who I smiled at when we first arrived. Now I knew why her eyes had been red. I ran after the car and waved until I could no longer make out their faces, then I stopped and just stood there, shrinking into myself until I thought no one could see me.

CHAPTER THREE

'Hello.' A tentative voice behind me made me jump. I turned and saw the girl from before. She was pretty, with big dark eyes, dark skin, short afro hair and thin legs. She offered a shy smile. 'Are you new? I saw you when you came with your parents. My name is Affiong, but you can call me Affie. What is your name?'

'Karina,' I offered a shaky smile, 'Nice to meet you, Affie.' Mum said I must never forget my manners, no matter where I am.

Affie looked at me curiously. She didn't say she was pleased to meet me too, but she tugged at my arm so we could walk back to the hostel.

'I just started here. I used to go to Holy Rosary School, but my sister, Eka, was here so my parents moved me. Eka is in Form Four. I'm in Primrose House, what about you?'

'Me too - I transferred from FGGC but I wanted to change schools, so my parents let me come here.'

'From FGGC to *Livingstone*? You must be mad!' There was no response to give, so she carried on talking.

For someone who looked so shy, she could talk a lot, but as I listened to her talk about her family and gossip about the names she'd heard about from Eka, I realised that I was not so scared of being here. I had made a new friend.

We quickly settled into a new routine of rising early, saying prayers and going to the dining hall for breakfast before going to our classrooms for the day. Affie and I were in the same hostel and it didn't take very long for us to realise that washing before everyone else woke up was the smart thing to do if we wanted to avoid being picked on by senior students to fill their buckets with water. Anyone who didn't have a shower before the prayer bell had to wait until after morning prayers to use the bathroom and then came daily chores. If you were lucky, your job was to attend the flowers in the courtyard. If someone hated you or your school mother wasn't powerful, you got toilet duty. Disgusting.

One day when I was late getting out of the dormitory, I was spotted by one a prefect. 'You there, Karina, come here,' she called me over to her. 'Take this bucket and fill it.' She handed me a metal bucket that was almost as big as me. It hurt to carry that bucket when it was full of water and my arm felt like it was going to fall off. After that day, I always got up before morning bell.

After the bell, we were given fifteen minutes to make our beds before 'devotion,' where we all had to show up, sing from our *Sacred Songs and Solos* hymn books and say our prayers together. We sang reluctantly and did our best not to fall asleep as Prefect Susannah prayed loudly for God to forgive our many sins. I think she really used the opportunity to talk to her classmates from the side of her mouth, pretending that she was talking to God. I liked Prefect Susannah because she was one of the nicer senior students, but her prayers were so long and boring. One day, while she was asking God to help Ma'Sei, the school cook prepare better tasting food, poor Gloria fell asleep. Gloria was in my class and her falling asleep was not so remarkable, but on the day in question, she fell onto one of the other students and interrupted the prayers. We laughed so hard and got punished for laughing, but how grateful we were that at least for that day, morning prayers were over.

After dressing up, we would straighten up our corners ready for inspection and then take our plates to the food hall for what was loosely described as breakfast. Again we quickly learned that if we were late, our tummies would go empty and growl loudly until lunchtime. There was barely time to rush back to the hostel and get our books, make sure our hair was neat, grey skirts and white blouses were tucked in and looking spotless, shoes were polished and socks were at the same height before heading out to assembly, and surprise inspections. It was relentless, but we soon got the hang of the daily rhythm and learned to pack as much fun into the time we had between lunch, siesta, prep and lights out.

At weekends, we had more time to ourselves, and those who had guardians in school went to have lunch in the teachers' quarters. Visiting day was once a month, but if you were sick, you could get a pass or 'exeat' to go home for the day. Affie and I pretended to be sick once so we could get an exeat, but the House Mistress knew we were pretending, so she made us weed her garden as punishment and sent us back empty-handed.

On Sunday evenings we had nothing to do, so we would gather around the window of Miss Mabibi's house and try to catch a glimpse of whatever was on television. Some students got into trouble for doing that.

In the early days of that first term, I spent a lot of time thinking about home. I was fine in the day, but as the night settled in and the lights went out, my arms would ache for want of a hug, and I would take out Mum's scarf that I had hidden in my case and press it to my nose. If I inhaled deeply, I could almost feel her with me in the dark. Sometimes I would talk to Daniel quietly, telling him about my day and pretending he could hear me. When one girl started calling me crazy for talking to someone I couldn't see, I took to hiding in the box room. Talking to my brother comforted me.

One day Senior Juliet found me hiding in the box room one day, crying.

'Karina, is that you?' Concern furrowed her eyebrows as she put her arm around me and pulled me to my feet, 'What's wrong? Why are you crying?'

My sobs grew even louder as her kindness gave me license to give in to my tears. 'I want to go ho-hooome,' I sobbed, 'I want my mum and my brother. I miss them.'

To my amazement, she laughed at me. 'Is that all? *That's why you're crying*?' She shook her head. 'I thought something bad had happened. *Oya* wipe your tears and don't cry anymore. You can come to my room and write a letter home, and I will ask one of the day students to help you drop it at home.'

I gulped back the rest of my tears and stared at her with wide eyes. 'Really? Can you really help me send a letter home?' The postal service didn't work well in Port Harcourt, and any letter I posted would probably get there at the end of the term.

She chuckled, '*Ajẹ bota*! Rich man pikin. You're so spoiled. Of course, you can write home. Just come to me and I will help you send it to your parents. That's one perk of being my school daughter.' She led me to her bedroom and installed me at a desk in the corner, shoving a pen and some note paper in front of me. 'Once you're done writing, you can go to bed - it's almost time for lights out. But you're a big girl now, so no more of all this crying. Enjoy your friends. We're only here for a few weeks and then we will go home.

And besides, your mummy will probably come to visit next weekend.'

After then, I wrote home every week and told Daniel about school life. I told him about Ma'Sei's cooking and the day the principal marched into the dining hall, insisting that the cooks serve us regular portions of fruit from the school farm. I told him that although we got pineapples that first day, we got no more fruit after that. I told him about Gloria falling asleep in prayer and in class, and about being punished for talking back to a prefect. I asked about Preye and whether Mum and Dad missed me, but I didn't ask him about the bitch. No matter how much I missed home, thinking about her always cured me instantly. No, I decided, being in school was better.

One day, after siesta, I went to the classroom to do my homework. As I walked past the Ixora hedges near the principal's office, I heard someone call my name.

'Karina. Karina!' I looked around, but seeing no one, I carried on walking until I heard footsteps running up to me.

'Karina?' The girl who caught up with me looked vaguely familiar, but I couldn't place her.

'Yes?'

'Hi, I just saw you walking and said I should join you. My name is Rhoda.'

'Good evening,' I was unsure of who she was or what she wanted. 'Sorry, but who are you?'

'My name is Rhoda. I'm in Bluebell House, and I'm in Form three. You're not in trouble oh, I just want to walk with you a little. I think you and I could be friends.' She smiled gently and walked me to my class, talking as we went and offering to come back to wait for me so we could walk to the dorm together. A little flattered to have been noticed by a senior student, I couldn't wait to tell Affie, who had gone ahead of me to class.

'*Hian*! Rhoda came to friend you?' Affie's reaction was not what I was expecting. She clapped her warning at me and tugged at her ear, 'Hmm! Better stay away from her oh! That one is looking for a new wife.'

I'd heard of some girls who went to 'befriend' younger girls to make them their "wives" and I certainly wasn't going to be anybody's wife, so Affie and I left before Rhoda came back. We agreed that I should tell Senior Juliet so she could protect me if Rhoda became vindictive, which we'd heard happened sometimes. When I wrote to Daniel the following week, I told him of my shock and horror when I went looking for Senior Juliet and found her busy with a wife of her own.

It was shocking, but it wasn't bad. The midterm break came soon, and the rest of the term passed without event. I learned to fight back when I was teased and to stop being afraid of everything. The test would come when I went home, but for now, I congratulated myself for making the right decision.

CHAPTER FOUR

Happy chaos reigned in the dormitory on the last day of term. We were officially done with our first year at secondary school and relieved to be going home. Girls called out gaily to one another across the courtyard as suitcases, boxes and bags were packed up for the summer holiday. Some of us had brought our mattresses in to school and had to haul them off to be locked up in the 'box room' to avoid having them stolen while everyone was away. The school mattresses were flat as pancakes and stunk of urine after years of use and abuse by the boarders who came through year after year, so no one cared if they were stolen.

The anticipation of change filled every corner. Celebratory cubes of sugar and scoops of bournvita and powdered milk were shared by those of us lucky enough to still have some provisions in our lockers.

I thought how empty the dorm would be and paused my flurry of activity to watch as friends and nemeses started to leave together, groups of friends moving as one but travelling in different directions. The chattering would no doubt include gossiping about the male teacher who was caught in a darkened corner with a student and the senior students who were caned in assembly for cheating in the WAEC exams only last week.

Everyone seemed to buzz with the excitement of going home because home meant six whole weeks where we didn't have to endure Ma'Sei's cooking. No more soups watered down to a thin gruel with barely nine or ten pieces of tinned fish floating around in the tureen, looking like victims of an oil spill. It hardly ever seemed enough to feed the twenty of us assigned to each table. The senior girls always came in and helped themselves before we had even said 'the grace', leaving the rest of us with hardly enough to fill our starving bellies.

Going home meant that mealtimes were eaten with civilised people who didn't fight over the tureens to keep their bellies full.

Best of all, we could have plates of hot, steaming *moimoi or akara* that were enough to fill us and *akamu* that tasted like it had actually been cooked. Far better than the daily stale bread here. My brother often said that *akamu* was Nigeria's answer to custard, but I thought it was better because you could almost taste the fresh corn from which it had been milled before being soaked and cooked into porridge. As a child, fresh *akamu* with a dash of evaporated milk and one cube of sugar tasted like a brand-new morning full of possibilities. And watching the black-eyed beans being ground, seasoned and steamed to make the *moimoi*, or fried to make *akara* was a thing of magic to me.

Home also meant each moment was not dictated by the ever-present bells: the morning bell to wake us up, prayer bell, bath time bell, mealtimes, games, periods, siesta, prep, and bedtime.

The sound of a school holiday song filled my ears. '*Holiday is coming, holiday is coming, no more morning bell, no more teacher's whip; Goodbye teachers, scholars goodbye, I am going to spend my jolly ho-li-day, my jolly ho-li-day!'* girls sang loudly as they headed off, arms linked. I watched them go, amused by their jollity and wishing I was as excited about going home as they were.

'Karina!' I jumped as I heard Senior Juliet call my name. I hadn't heard her behind me. 'Are you daydreaming again, you this girl?'

Senior Juliet often reprimanded me for my constant daydreaming, because daydreaming was the privilege of white people and *aje-botas* – spoiled and privileged children of well-off parents. If only she knew.

'You'd better hurry up,' she said, 'I think I just saw your driver outside.'

And with that reminder, I zipped up my bag and shoved my bucket in my locker for safe keeping.

'Bye Senior Juliet!' I called as I sped out through the side door, my suitcase banging against the door frame. I didn't wait for her to say, 'Greet your mummy for me.' I would greet her anyway.

I ran all the way across the sandy quadrangle to the dorm gates before I slowed down. The dormitories I passed stood low and long, with two wings for each house which were linked at one end, forming a right angle so that there was one set of shared bathrooms and box rooms for the girls. Bluebell and Primrose Houses occupied the same space, each one placed on the outside of a quadrangle. By the gate there was a small, double-room accommodation where our cook Ma'Sei lived. She was old and looked after us like a mother hen.

She hailed me as I ran past, asking in her preferred pidgin if I was leaving, '*Ehen, my pikin, you don dey go 'ouse?*'

'Yes ma,' I said. I slowed down but didn't stop.

'*You say wetin?* What did you say?' The old hen also couldn't hear well.

Loudly this time, I said 'Yes ma, I'm going home now'

'*Ehen! My pikin go well, ihia*?' The fact that she said "ihia" in place of 'you hear' always amused me. Like it was a single word.

I didn't answer her this time. There was nothing more to say.

Passing the gates, I spotted Edet, my parent's driver, immediately. My heart sank because he was my least favourite driver – I preferred Ade. Edet was a short, stern man. His unsmiling face made him difficult to relate with, but his love for safari suits made him the butt of our daily jokes and incessant teasing at home. He stood by the pale blue Peugeot 504 he often drove, looking impatiently at his wristwatch. Heaving a sigh, I trudged the rest of the way to the car, wishing it had been someone else Mum had sent to pick me up.

'Edet, good afternoon,' I said automatically.

'Afternoon Karina, how are you?' he asked. Then without waiting for an answer, he continued, 'Come on now, *hurry up, I have been waiting for a while. Mummy will be annoyed if we stayed longer.'*

He took my suitcases from me and dumped them in the boot of the car. Slumping into my seat, my small hands searched the glove compartment, hoping to find something to read that would take my mind off the giant knot that had taken up residence in the pit of my stomach.

I came up empty. I looked at my hands, incredulous, feeling oddly betrayed by their emptiness.

'*Na wetin you dey find?*' Edet's voice startled me. When had he climbed into the driver's seat? 'What are you looking for?' he repeated in English when I didn't respond immediately.

'Nothing,' I sighed heavily, 'I was looking for a book to read.' As we slowly made our way out of the school gates and joined the flow of the famous Port Harcourt traffic, my mind drifted alongside the car as my body sat trapped in a tin can.

I wondered what 'adventures' Daniel would have planned for us this summer. My brother always had something up his sleeve, which made him exciting to be around. Mum called our escapades foolishness and said we would break our necks one day, but that didn't stop Preye and I following our big brother into everything like the three musketeers.

The anticipation of being with my siblings was only slightly dulled by the face that rose next to my mind. 'Yuck!' I spat the word out like a bad taste, the way I saw Ma'Sei spitting out the pulp of her chewing stick every morning. Of all the nannies we'd ever had, *she* was definitely the worst. She had a secret that only I knew. She was a witch and the reason my feet dragged a little, instead of running home like my friends.

At some point along the way home, I started playing a game with myself – counting the number of Mercedes Benz cars I could find. I counted the blue and silver ones only. There is only one rule – blue cars meant I would take the biggest gamble my twelve-year-old self could imagine; silver cars meant… I don't know. I just wanted my mind to stop running around in crazy circles whenever I thought of the bitch and her secret, looping around and out of control while I watched it like a spectator.

CHAPTER FIVE

Karina, 2017

I sigh as I recall the ride home. It was raining as we made our way home, making the usual Port Harcourt traffic even worse and forcing us to leave the main road and cut through the much quieter Government Residential Area to get home. GRA was a nice part of town with grand houses and good roads, and we lived on the edge of it. It's amazing the things the mind remembers - the group of children playing in the rain seemingly without a care in the world, the potholes on Onne Road, the sound of the rain falling. Funny how whenever I think of that day, the one thing I remember is the patter of the rain drops, the feeling that my skin would desert me because it could not contain the crazy rhythm of my heart which was beating away faster and faster until I couldn't breathe anymore and I thought I would surely die from the fear that had me in its grip. Funny how I never think of myself as afraid. I don't remember thinking as much as just *being*. I don't recall thinking about seeing my brother whom I adored so completely, or my little sister Preye whom I had missed sorely, even though I'm sure I was eager to see them.

Instead my mind was focused on that monster who lived with my family and pretended to be human. Her presence was to me like an oppressive, dark advancement of vitriol. She who wore a smile and went to church every Sunday and gave me and my sister sweets and pieces of meat from the pot. Oh, I didn't think of her consciously; in fact, everything I did on that trip was calculated to ensure she never made it to the front of my mind. But she was there. In the patter of the rain, the curve of the pepper seller's hip, the swag in the step of the girl who sold sugarcane…

I pluck a blade of grass and pop it in my mouth, vaguely conscious that Mum would have a fit if she saw me doing that.

CHAPTER SIX

Karina, 1997

Colourful bougainvillea in shades of purple and orange jostled for space and spilled over the top of the fence, signalling that we were pulling up to the gate. As the car pulled into the compound, I shook myself a little to clear my head. I was home. Who would guess that I was only here a few short weeks ago, it felt foreign and familiar at the same time.

I emerged from the car and paused to take in the familiar scents and sounds of the compound; the different plants vying for space and attention in the front yard, the soft tinkling of the wind chimes that reminded me of many afternoons spent running around. Dad had repainted the house. It looked like the grey of the sky before a thunderstorm.

I walked around the side of the house to the back door – the front door was for important visitors - dragging my luggage behind me and doing my best to avoid the potted palms that lined the narrow walkway. The door flew open and Preye barrelled into me with a squeal, squeezing me tight, 'Karina! You're home!'

Daniel was close on her heels, but he was too cool to run. We hi-fived and grinned at each other for a few seconds before he took my bag from me.

'Finally! I thought you guys would never get here. How now?'

'Fine, thanks. There was traffic on the way, you know how it gets.'

We are joined by the house girls, Patience and Comfort who came out to say hello and make a fuss. Already, I felt myself being enveloped by the warmth of their familiar faces and voices as we moved our little party indoors.

'*Chei* Karina!' Comfort grabbed my arm and poked at my ribs, 'see as you lean. You've lost so much weight! Don't they feed you in that school? *Come. Come and eat,*' she ushered me into the kitchen. '*I done fry plantain and eggs for you.*' Comfort was the older of our two house girls and a natural feeder.

My mouth literally watered. I was so hungry for the taste of home.

I looked around quickly as she grabbed my hand and pulled me into the kitchen, dishing up a plate of food before I'd even had the chance to change out of the school uniform that hung from my now skinny frame. I washed my hands and eagerly dug into the heaping plate of home-cooked food.

My mouth savoured each bite, but somehow my mind and soul had wandered off. Like I was ten feet away from my body, watching me eat and talk at the same time.

After I'd stuffed myself and changed out of my uniform, I played with Preye, chatted with Daniel, and teased Dad when he got home from work all with an eerie sense of detachment. I knew it was a matter of time before it all fell apart.

Preye happily followed me about the house all afternoon. Her big sister was back and we played happily for the rest of the day. Mum had not come back from work, even though Edet had left to pick her up ages ago, and I was disappointed that she didn't rush home to see me.

I was reading a novel when I heard her voice through the open window. She announced her return from the market and chatted with Patience about the price of fabric. Reprieve over, my heart started to pound in my ears, loud and irregular, but I barely heard it. I noticed the book in my hand shaking like an old person was holding it, rather than me. She had returned home.

My ears followed her noisy approach, and I smelled her before I saw her.

'Ah Karina, you're back from school?'

Forcing myself to look up, I muttered a 'good afternoon' under my breath. Even my ears struggled to hear me, but let no one say I didn't greet her.

'Is that all I get from you? Greet me well now.'

I looked again at her permed hair, thick lips and the weird black lines she had drawn where her eyebrows used to be.

'Ebele,' I hissed her name under my breath. She had a stupid smile and I delighted in watching it drop to a frown as my eyes began to drop to my book without offering the greeting she asked for. She stood there and gaped as I started singing softly in pidgin English, 'Ebele the bitch. Ebele the bitch. Ebele carry *kpondo.' Kpondo* – last place, loser, useless, reduced, less, a nobody. I knew it would infuriate her because she often told the other house girls that she was better than them. That she wasn't just a maid. But she was worse. She was a rat!

The evening sped by too quickly, gathered as we were in the living room with the TV on. God, I hated that music they played just before the nine o'clock NTA news – '*puhn puhn puuun, puhn pihn paraaa*.' It trumpeted the news that all children must go to bed. In fact, we didn't even have to wait for Dad to peer over his glasses and point at us while saying 'Bed!' If you knew what was good for you, you got up quietly, said goodnight and went to your room. As for me, I always grumbled because I never wanted to go to bed.

The only good part was pulling my favourite nightie over my head – the pale blue one with a tiger on the front. The material felt soft, thin, and bobbled from too much washing. Mum said it was getting too small for me, but I refused to part with it. Nkiru the tiger prowled strong and fierce. She made me feel bold, and in my imagination, I was just as powerful as that tiger.

I lay awake for a long time, listening to the sounds of the house. Lying still under my blanket, I listened to the dogs barking as they were let out of their kennels to roam in the dark, my parents laughing and chatting softly as they sipped their tea and listened to John Momoh and Tokunbo Ajayi read the nightly news. I listened until everything was quiet, and the house hushed its stirring, straining my ears until all that was left to me was the sound of the clock, ticking the minutes away. Every single sound the house made as it fell asleep was familiar. I knew them because after the day had drained away, I would lie awake waiting and thinking that maybe this would be the night, only to find out in the morning that it wasn't.

Waiting, thinking, and wondering always amused me. I would play games in my head, have conversations and confidently make friends with people I didn't know. In my mind, I could be angry and shout at that witch Ebele; I would hiss at her and abuse her. My little mind called her a foolish, useless woman. Imagining giving her the 'bad eye' while holding my nose from her stench - she always smelt of dried sweat and onions – brought such satisfaction.

Ebele was a bad woman, the kind we used to hear about that would bribe children with *agbalumo* before killing them for rituals. My English teacher tried to get us to call *agbalumo* by its English name - White Star Apple - but that made the whole class laugh until we got punished. White star apple indeed. I shook my head at the memory.

I hated Ebele. That was my secret. No one knew how much I hated her. She embarrassed me because she was the local *ashewo*. Prostitute. Loose woman. Women used to come and fight with her on our street. They would clap their hands in her face and tear her clothes because she followed their husbands and boyfriends, but Mum never knew. She thought Ebele did a good job looking after me and my sister, but sometimes Ebele took us when she visited her man friends, and we had to watch them 'play wrestling'. Preye didn't watch because I covered her eyes or tried to distract her with cartoons or a story.

'Why do you have to remove your clothes to play?' I had asked. When she tired of my questions, Ebele would slap my face and shout at me.

'*Sharrap*! Stupid girl,' her lips would curl, making her even uglier than normal. She couldn't even say 'shut up' correctly. 'You ask stupid questions because you're fat and lazy.'

At first, it puzzled me and I had wondered what my being fat had to do with the question I asked her. After all, the people on TV every Saturday in WWF wrestling matches fought with their clothes on.

I hated Ebele for many reasons. I hated her because she called me names and stole our TV time, dragging us off to one place or the other when Mum was out. I hated her because she made me feel small, afraid and desperate all at once. Did I mention that she smelled?

One day, she heard my brother calling her a bitch and she reported him to my Mum, who gave him six strokes of the cane. I sneaked into his room to say sorry when no one was looking. I didn't know what a 'bitch' was, but it sounded right because it sounded like 'witch', which she definitely was.

'Ebele the bitch, Ebele the bitch...' I sang to myself in the dark, thinking of the glee with which I hugged that little song to myself when no one was listening.

'Ebele … you go carry *kpondo*,' a giggle escaped my lips and I quickly covered my mouth as my sister began to stir.

My eyes counted the ceiling tiles as I listened to my sister's breathing slowly deepen again. By the time I counted to a hundred, she was fast asleep.

CHAPTER SEVEN

Karina, 2017

The soft sound of purposeful footsteps reaches into my trance and brings me firmly back to the present. I don't look up from my spot on the grass where he left me, feeling instead his sharp gaze on me. He waits for a heartbeat before dropping to his haunches to investigate my face.

'Hi Akin,' I said.

'Hey you,' he says gently, 'What are you still doing here? Your mum called me. She's getting a little worried. Are you hurt?'

I lift my left hand to look at my wristwatch, more than a little surprised at the time that has passed since Akin left me. My mother would be fretting, but the wedding was not until four o'clock. Delaying my hairdresser doesn't bother me. Akin has showered and changed into a pair of khaki trousers, and has swapped his trainers for a pair of brown loafers. His brown polo shirt nearly melts into his dark brown skin.

I shake my head; my voice seems to have disappeared altogether.

'Okay. You said you would leave here "in fifteen minutes". I went home, had a shower and stopped by your house to drop off Daniel's shoes for the wedding, only to find out that you were still gone. Karina you must tell me what's happening. I don't imagine you're having second thoughts about marrying Tosan, so what's up?'

I look down at my hands, both laid flat against the grass beside me. Akin's eyes follow mine, and he exhales impatiently. 'Wait. Are you having second thoughts?'

No answer.

'Karina, please you're scaring the shit out of me,' he's pleading now, hand on my knee. Slowly, my eyes meet his, *knowing* it would probably be my undoing. I try biting the inside of my cheek to keep myself from crying but lose the battle as my eyes fill with tears.

'Yes,' I whisper as I bury my head in my hands, engulfed by emotions. My throat almost seals shut as it aches. My skin feels like a thousand ants are crawling over me. Squinting my eyes shut, I wish that I could curl into a ball and disappear.

But of course, I don't disappear. Instead, I hear myself sobbing as though my heart would break, my voice like shattered glass, fractured, broken and scattered across the field. Akin pulls me into his arms and rocks me from side to side, kissing my forehead and making unintelligible, soothing noises, waiting for the tsunami of tears to subside. He presses his handkerchief into my clenched fists before pulling me into another tight embrace.

'That'll do now, Karina,' his voice anchors me, 'it will be alright. *Oya* stop wailing like a local girl.

People will wonder what I'm doing to you here.' His attempt at humour does little to quiet me, but somewhere in my mind, a little calm begins to be restored.

My ugly crying - complete with rocking - and snot on my face should faze him, but it doesn't. Even in my state, the fact that he takes it in his stride doesn't escape my subconscious notice. Right now, he just holds me against his broad chest until my sobbing peters out into a less violent expression of whatever it is that's going on with me.

Long minutes pass before I become aware of the sounds in the air around us, the heat that's growing as the sun climbs higher and higher, and the snot I've covered Akin's clean shirt in. How safe and comfortable I feel in his arms as he continues to make those comforting sounds, stopping only to plant a kiss on my temple.

'You can let go of me now,' I say with a hiccup.

Akin chuckles, lets go of me, and nudges the hand that's still holding the handkerchief he had given me. 'Clean your face up girl,' he teases gently, 'you look a hot mess! In fact, I should take a picture to show my kids someday - the day Aunty Karina looked less than her best!'

I roll my eyes while a smile teases its way onto my face.

'Ah, she's smiling! Thank God.' Akin's wide smile shows his relief and his eyes probe mine. 'Do you want to tell 'Uncle Akin' about it?' he asks as he settles himself down beside me.

For a few more seconds, I battle my inner demons and try to count the cost of baring it all. Being strong has always been my thing. That's my shield, my mask. I'm strong therefore I'm invincible. Telling him the truth will take that away from me. Then again, how well has being strong worked out for me so far. In that moment, my decision is made as I open my mouth and words tumble out.

'Being strong has always been my thing,' the words come easily. 'It's my shield. You've asked me repeatedly why I'm so driven to run, work hard, play hard. I think today is the day to give you some answers. I want to stop running.'

So, I tell him about Ebele.

CHAPTER EIGHT

Karina, 1997

The air conditioner hummed, sounding rather like Mallam Bukio after he had drunk out of his 'special bottle,' which he thought nobody knew about. He was the gateman; he was supposed to man the gate and not let strangers in, but Mallam Bukio did not work well when he drank from his bottle. Last summer he fell asleep and didn't hear when Uncle Eddie came to see Dad. Uncle Eddie pressed his horn for ten minutes, but Mallam didn't open the gate, so he left. Getting his fingers attacked by the dogs wasn't worth trying to open the gate himself.

When Dad found out, he was a step away from anger, but he didn't sack Mallam. Instead, he fixed him with a long and piercing glare until Mallam began studying the floor. He studied it so intently, you would have thought he expected to have an exam about the terrazzo pattern afterwards. Kaine and I had stood just out of sight, wickedly enjoying the sight of poor Mallam squirming whilst we waited for the line we just knew Dad would deliver next. We had hardly been able to contain ourselves, because for some inane reason, the words always made us giggle helplessly.

Dad always delivered in the same way. He would say it so slowly and loudly, as if the person was a little hard of hearing and could only hear in slow motion. Every single word would be drawn out and delivered with great sadness. Dad would shake his head sadly, simultaneously managing to look disturbed, disgusted, sad and shocked at the level of idiocy and stupidity in the offending human being. It was an art form, and you felt the pain of the person he was talking to because their face said they felt just as stupid as he made them out to be.

Kaine counted down with her fingers. At one, we heard it.

'Mallam Bukiioooo,' Dad fixed poor Mallam with his super "bad eye". 'Whaaat is the matter with yoouu? *Ehn*?'

Poor Mallam looked like he wished he could just melt. Kaine and I had run away, laughing so hard by this time, we nearly wet ourselves. We couldn't say 'God punish you!' when he refused to open the gate for our friends - Mum didn't allow us to say things like that - but we certainly could laugh at him when God *did* punish him.

My teeth glowed in the dark of my room, and I wondered now if God would punish Ebele for her wickedness. Or punish me for mine.

Ebele came to live with us last year. I just finished Primary five and was looking forward to starting secondary school. One Saturday after swimming, me and Daniel heard snatches of Mum's conversation with Dad, although we paid no real attention. Words like 'focus', 'grow' and 'help' were uttered, but who cared? But we should have cared, because later we would find out that Mum's promotion at work meant we needed a nanny.

While doing our homework, we heard a knock at the door, accompanied by a bright voice, '*kpom kpom.*' As if the door was incapable of making its own sound. Me and Daniel looked up at each other and craned our necks to see who it was.

'*Na who be dat?*' Patience's voice sounded angry, like someone had just interrupted a very important job she was doing, but she was only watching telly with Preye. 'Who is that knocking?'

'Hello, please I'm looking for Mrs Thompson.'

'*Wetin* be your name?' Dan looked at me and shrugged. Patience was usually polite, but she wasn't this time. Maybe she knew something.

'Ebele Okafor' the woman flashed a nervous smile and patted her hair. She wore a plain blue dress and her hair was plaited in big cornrows that hung long at the back.

'Mummy *dey* inside. Wait, let me go call her. Did she tell you to come?'

'Yes. My sister said I should come this afternoon, that madam would be expecting me.' She spoke better than Patience with her broken English.

'Okay, sit here,' she pointed to a chair on the veranda and walked off.

That evening Mum and Dad told us that we were getting a new helper.

'But why? We already have Comfort and Patience.' Preye looked as confused as I felt.

'Well, she's more like a nanny than a maid,' Mum responded, 'I'm going to be a bit busier with work and I need somebody here who can look after you and your sister when I can't be here. Okay?'

'But what about Dad?'

I rolled my eyes. 'Looking after children is a woman's job, Preye. Don't you know anything?'

There was nothing to discuss. We welcomed her into our home and it was great at first. Ebele was a lot of fun. She made jokes with us, taught us new games and with our friends. She even joined in our games of hide and seek or police and thieves. None of the other adults did that, and it was fun. Sometimes she went out in the afternoon when she was supposed to be looking after me and Preye, but she didn't stay for too long. Ebele took us to Mr Biggs fast foods when Mum couldn't, and to Domino supermarket to buy sweets.

But sometimes, after giving me sweets, she would poke me in my tummy and say I should stop eating or I would soon look like an elephant. One time when I annoyed her, she locked me in the toilet for hours and said she didn't know where I was. She confused me because she was nice to everybody and went *to Assemblies of God* church. But she lied and if I said she was lying, she would pinch me. She told Osita and Kaine not to play with me sometimes, because I would spoil them, but Kaine didn't listen. I wanted to be Ebele's friend because everybody liked her, and maybe everybody was sometimes mean. But when she came to my room for the first time, I knew she wasn't just mean. She was a wicked woman.

When Ebele came into my room that night, I was ready. Sort of. I heard a faint sound outside my room door. Her smell wafted into my nostrils before she had fully entered the room. As I waited for her eyes to become accustomed to the darkness, I prepared my next move.

She opened and shut the door very quietly, sneaking in like the worm she was. As she felt her way around the room, I strengthened my resolve with thoughts of how much I despised her. *Kai!* I knew that God would punish me because Uncle Akpan, my Sunday school teacher, used to say 'Don't hate anybody. Hate is the devil's work'.

I retrieved the razor-sharp knife I had hidden under my pillow, thinking back to the start of that day and how reluctant I was to come home for the holiday. Well, this would be the day that something would change. Just holding the knife gave me some comfort, and I kissed it and breathed a quick prayer for help before returning it to its hiding place.

I closed my eyes tight and lay as still as I could. The element of surprise would be the only thing I had on my side, after all she was bigger and much stronger than I was. My fear rushed a need to use the toilet, and I prayed to God that my bladder would not let me down before I got the chance to show this woman some serious pepper. 'God,' trying to communicate with him in my mind, 'if you are awake, please can you help me not to wet my bed?'

I wondered if God would answer me, or if he was asleep just like my parents. God always seemed to be asleep whenever Ebele came, because he never answered my prayer to make her stop.

My visions of skilfully slicing her throat in one move like James Bond suddenly dimmed, and I realised perhaps I should have planned a bit better, because now that her musty smell and ugly face loomed over me, I didn't know what to do. I opened my eyes and met hers in the darkness. Darkness and anger oozed from her face, probably because I'd called her the bad 'B' word today. She leaned down and whispered in my ear, her hand already reaching for the hem of my nightie.

'So Karina, I have been waiting for you to come home all this time, and instead of greeting me well, you started calling me names. I will show you what a bitch is today, you foolish girl!'

A struggle ensued as I fought to reclaim the hem of my nightie and stop her wandering hands from grabbing me so roughly. She laughed as she overpowered me, gleeful as a whimper rose in my throat, knife and bravado quite forgotten. 'Please Ebele, I'm sorry. Please don't. I won't do it again.'

I promised her anything I could think of. I would be good, wash my plate after eating my food and not talk back. I promised all my pocket money and said I wouldn't call her bad names anymore. 'Just please, I'm begging you, please leave me alone.'

'*Sharrap, my fren,*' she hissed at me to shut up. 'If you make any noise, I will tell your mummy how rotten you are inside. She thinks you're a good girl, but I will tell her you're bad and you know that she will beat you well.'

Her words awoke my spirit. When Rhoda bullied me for refusing to be her 'friend', Affie said, "*All die na die*, Karina - just make sure you go down fighting. If you let her, she will make your life miserable forever in this school. Fight back…" And I did. If I could deal with Rhoda, then I could do the same here. My blubbering and begging ceased as I realised it would make no difference. My detachment from earlier in the day returned and I reached and pulled out the knife from its hiding place under my pillow and held it's tip to her cheek. She stilled.

'Touch me again and die, Ebele. In fact, let us wake Mum now, because just as you want to tell her something, I too have something to tell her.' I didn't bother to whisper, no longer caring whether or not I woke Preye. I felt eerily calm. Something whispered to me that I had nothing to lose and nothing to fear.

Ebele's eyes widened, and her hands ceased their worrying of my hemline as it slowly dawned on her what was happening. Although she backed away, I could make out the daggers her eyes were shooting at me, and the ugly twist of her lips as she sneered. '*Ehn* Karina? Really? Is it me you want to *chook* with a knife? You want to stab me? I will show you who is who in this house!'

Feeling brave for the first time, I could finally laugh in her face. 'Show me? *Oya* show me now. I will wait, but I'm not afraid of you anymore,' I derided, my voice growing stronger, 'God will punish you. You witch!'

As she turned and stumbled from my bedroom for the last time, I looked in amazement at the knife in my hand and wished I had befriended that orange-handled blade a lot earlier. I slid it back under my pillow and waited for sleep to claim me.

#

Dear Diary:

When Ebele first came to our house, I liked her a lot because I thought she was pretty and very nice. She plaited her hair with extensions to make it look like Bob Marley. She spoke good English, not like Comfort who is always speaking in pidgin English, even though Mum tells her not to. Ebele treated me like a big girl and allowed me to go to Domino Stores on my own. She said she liked my green dress with the hearts on it and let me stay with her when she was dressing up so that I could hear her talk about her boyfriend. Ebele has had many boyfriends, and she told me about kissing.

I've only seen oyinbo *people kissing on the TV, and it surprised me that she had done it because she is not white like them. Uncle Samson used to shout at the people on TV to 'Stop it!' whenever they started kissing, so I thought that it was a bad thing.*

I liked how she used to make us laugh and give me and Preye extra pieces of meat from the pot when Mum wasn't at home. I was surprised that she could play ten-ten with me and Kaine and beat us at it. I don't know any other grown-ups who can play ten-ten.

I liked her a lot and maybe she knew that. Maybe that's why she came to my room at night. When she first started coming to my room, I didn't understand what was happening, but I knew it was wrong for her to try to play with me like that. Mum would be angry with me if she knew, but Ebele said 'shhh, she will only be annoyed if she knows.' I wish she had just wanted to play ten-ten.

Now I want to tell you my secret about Ebele. I know I shouldn't tell a secret to anybody, but I have to tell. I think it is my fault that Ebele did the thing she did to me.

She said that if I tell, she would tell Mum that I was the one who started it. She said no one would believe me anyway, but when she saw me crying, she promised to give me buttermint sweets. Maybe she was afraid that somebody would hear me.

Sometimes when she comes to my room, I would pretend that I was asleep. The first time she woke me up by pulling my clothes off, but after that she either slapped or pinched me hard until I cried out.

Uncle Akpan said that the devil doesn't have any family. He's alone and that is why he looks for people to take to hell with him. But I don't think Uncle Akpan has met Ebele, because he would know that she is the devil's sister.

One day she said that if I continued complaining, she would take my underwear away and show it to Osita. She said she would tell him I wet the bed, so that he wouldn't play with me anymore. She knows I like Osita.

Did I tell you that Mum warned me to tell my house mistress if any senior girl tried to touch me in a 'bad' way? I cried when she said that, and she thought I was afraid of going to school, but that wasn't why I cried. I was crying because Ebele was the bad one, and I didn't know how to tell.

Now that she has left me alone, maybe she will stay away. I hope she will. Or maybe she will punish me instead.

CHAPTER NINE

The next morning, I woke up disoriented. Everything felt different. From the soft big bed which was a far cry from my noisy and uncomfortable spring bed in school, to the sounds that filtered in with the morning sunlight and even the way the air smelled. Cracking one eye open, I slowly reminded myself of my surroundings – pale pink walls and the white wardrobe in the corner where Preye hid during every game of hide and seek – today, however, the wardrobe seemed smaller than I remembered.

I looked over at my sister's bed, unsurprised to find it empty. Preye was an early riser and had probably wandered to the kitchen for her drink of Milo, which was her morning ritual.

Had I been at school, I'd have already rushed off to have a wash whilst it was still dark before the morning bell for class. All the junior students did our best to get up before the first bell, so we could avoid the call to 'Go and fetch me water, toad.'

The familiar sounds of family life filtered through the window, bringing me back to my bedroom. I heard the bustle of activity. The house had come alive while I was sleeping in. Mallam Bukio was washing the cars, Ime was watering the plants which Mum had painstakingly planted in every part of the compound that wasn't paved. Domestic workers and early visitors called out cheerful greetings to one another, '*Una* good morning oh!' was met with '*Ehen*! Morning my brother (or sister)! How now?'

In the distance, I could hear someone calling for Patience, the house girl. Patience had a knack for disappearing for long periods with no real explanation. It puzzled me that so much time was spent looking for her every day, nor could I figure out why on earth we all called her Peshe.

'Peshe!' my cousin Kaine shouted, 'Paay-shaaay oh!' But there was no response. I was surprised to hear Kaine's voice because she hadn't been here yesterday. Her driver must have dropped her off this morning. Kaine was an only child and she spent a lot of time with me and my siblings. This was her second home.

'*Abeg, una see* Patience? Aunty dey find am,' that was Kaine asking no one in particular if they had seen Patience. I chuckled at the resignation in Kaine's voice. Some things never change and Peshe wouldn't be found until she was done hiding.

'No oh, I never see am,' that sounded like Ime.

'E be like say she go buy egg from Domino supermarket…' I tried but couldn't make out the voice. Not that it mattered.

They talked and laughed while I lay in my bed, wondering how they could be so oblivious. A heavy dread slowly crept across my limbs as I contemplated getting out of bed and facing Ebele. I couldn't believe what I had done, threatening her with a knife. My life wouldn't be worth living! Taking a deep breath to steady my galloping heart, I slowly reached under my pillow and felt for the handle of the knife I had left there. I needed to make sure it got back to the kitchen before anyone missed it. It was the 'good' knife, the sharpest one we had. I groped around for it, hoping for a small bit of comfort before I got out of bed to face the day, but instead my fingers closed around a small, crumpled up piece of paper. The knife was gone.

'What the hell?' I pulled out my hand and unfolded the paper, 'You are a folish gehl.' My mind struggled to comprehend, even as I noted the poor spelling. It had to be Ebele.

Any last vestiges of sleep instantly disappeared as I jumped out of bed and searched frantically. I lifted my pillow with an 'Ah-ah!' but no knife magically appeared. I knew my mind wasn't lying to me about putting it there after Ebele left. Quickly, I re-enacted the events that had gone before. My hand replayed every movement, pointing the knife at Ebele and gazing at my orange-handled friend in amazement before sliding it under my pillow for safekeeping. Convinced that I had missed it again, I threw the covers off my bed and shook them vigorously, hoping to hear the welcome clatter of metal hitting the floor. I flew over to Preye's bed and incautiously swept my hand under her pillow and covers, crawled around on my knees looking under the beds and furniture, while praying desperately that I would find that knife, but I searched in vain.

My body dropped heavily on my bed and I tried not to cry. The euphoria of having bested my tormentor completely evaporated. In a final frantic attempt, I stripped my bed, then my sister's, hoping against hope. Dresser drawers got dumped and the dirty clothes basket flew upside down and emptied.

The knife was gone. How could I have slept while Ebele or someone else came and took it from its hiding place under my pillow? Who else could have known?

My stomach sped like a roller coaster, churning nausea in my throat. The room spun wildly, and the

mouth remained slightly open, mirroring the look of dismay on Daniel's face.

'Daniel!' I wailed again, 'I'm in soup!'

Daniel was my partner in crime and my rock. With only eighteen months between us, we were more like twins than anything else.

My words shocked both of us – him because of what I said I did, and me because *hadn't I just said I wasn't telling anyone?!* Had an alien taken over my body to say the very thing I swore not to say to him?

My brother shook his head as if to clear his brain. 'Wait Karina, I don't understand. You did what?' his voice dropped to an urgent whisper, 'Did you say you took the knife from the kitchen to *stab Ebele?* Why on earth were you trying to stab Ebele? What did she do to you?' His forehead scrunched up, and he squinted his eyes as he tried to decide whether I was serious or making it up. 'Come, are you lying to me? Don't play with me like that Karina, what really happened?'

'Daniel, I'm not playing. Does my face look like the face of a person who is playing? I hate that

Ebele and I swear to God who made me, I will kill her one day if I can,' my small voice was a little wobbly but full of venom.

He looked at me like I was crazy,' okay… but why do you want to injure her? Never mind that you will be in trouble for it. What did she do to you?'

My head dropped in resignation as I shook my head. It was time to face the day. I knew he would hang around me until I told him what was going on, and I could draw strength from his presence. I wished I could take back the words that had inadvertently blurted out, but they had committed me now. A feeling of relief crept in that someone knew what the literal hell had been going on.

'Dan, let me get dressed before someone comes to find me. I will tell you after breakfast,' he looked hard at me, surveyed the room one last time, then nodded. His feet picked their way across the mess before he quietly shut the door behind him.

I took one last look around but couldn't find my orange-handled saviour. Hoping that just maybe Preye had somehow found it and taken it to the kitchen, I whispered a frantic prayer as I dressed and went for breakfast. Ebele walked past me in the parlour and said nothing. Was it possible that Ebele had left the note, but not taken the knife? It must be so. Convinced it was a sign that Preye took it, my spirits lifted and I wandered through the casual sitting room we called the 'small parlour' and into the more formal parlour to find my folks.

'*Serido* Mum, *serido* Dad,' I said good morning to my parents in our language and kissed them. That always made Dad happy. This room was sectioned into two sitting areas, the smaller area being made up of three high-backed armchairs and a marble table and phone console. This was where I found my parents, eating their customary bowls of freshly cut pineapples and pawpaw and drinking Earl Grey tea with homegrown lemon grass, which smelled divine. The smell of all that lovely fruit made my mouth water with sudden hunger.

'Mhmm,' came the response. Dad's mouth was full. '*Serido* my dear, how are you?'

'I'm fine, thanks Dad.'

He patted my shoulder twice, 'S*eri, seri*. Get up. Come and eat fruit with me.' He reached for his bowl of fruit, speared a juicy looking chunk of pineapple, and offered it to me. I ate happily, the juices slaking my thirst and drawing an answering grumble from my stomach.

Dad waved me to the empty chair and called for someone to bring an extra teacup and a bowl of fruits for me. Delighted at the fresh food, I happily sat down and chatted away about the happenings in school during the term, all thoughts of the missing knife put away. By the time I was describing how Mr. Barido punished a group of us for watching '*Willie Willie*' through the window of another teacher's house, Mum and Dad were in stitches. While chattering until my parents laughed, I was happy in a way that I had almost forgotten was possible at home. Being home felt good, basking in the warmth of my parents' attention. Only contentment existed here.

'Daddy, good morning sah,' Ebele's stupid voice shattered the moment, and for a second my lungs forgot their job.

'Yes, yes, good morning Ebele. How now? You sleep well?'

'I *dey* okay, Daddy. Fine thank you,' she answered, '*Mummy*, good morning ma.' Ebele had the nerve to smirk in my direction, which got her a scowl in return.

'Yes oh, Ebele. Morning. We've seen each other this morning, haven't we?'

'Yes ma,' she nodded before looking across at me. 'Karina, won't you say hello to me?'

I rolled my eyes and spat a 'good morning,' under my breath. In one second, she had sucked out all the pleasure from my morning, poisoning the air with her stench.

'*Haba*!' she clearly didn't know when to stop, 'are we fighting? Greet me well now.'

I eyed her from head to toe, taking in her slightly faded pink t-shirt, black skirt, and rubber slippers. Her hair was carefully done up in neat little cornrows in a hairstyle known locally as '*shabba*'– ever since Shabba Ranks became popular, every new hairstyle was *shabba* this and *shabba* that – I couldn't help the sneer that curled my lip. Mum and Dad were watching me, wondering what had happened to cause their usually docile daughter to behave so disrespectfully.

We locked eyes; a small smile played around her lips when I refused to blink until my eyes watered. If I backed down, I was finished. Her threats from the night before echoed in my brain, but I couldn't be the one to look away, no matter how scared I was. I think I peed on myself a little.

'Karina!' Mum's voice was sharp and a little impatient with my impudence. Disrespecting an adult was not acceptable in her house, no matter the circumstances. Even if they were the help. 'Can't you say good morning politely?'

'Mum, I already greeted her. If she doesn't like the greeting I gave her, let her buy 'good morning' from Mama Charlie in the village.' Mama Charlie was the local plantain seller who always stood ready with a cheerful greeting.

'Karina, what has come over you?' Now I knew I was testing Mum's patience.

Ebele oozed with false respect, 'Mum leave her, no problem. I think she's just getting used to being back home. By tomorrow she would have settled down and remembered how to talk, and the way we do things.' The veiled threat was enough for my appetite to abandon me.

CHAPTER TEN

'Sorry Mum,' I muttered, as I shrank into myself, mortified that I had offended my mother already. Hot tears burned my eyes, threatening to spill. Dad had tried to stay out of it, but as Ebele busied herself with receiving instructions from Mum for the day, he nudged my foot to get my attention. I looked up to see him wink slowly at me.

'Don't mind them *jare*,' he said jovially. 'Don't mind anybody. You've already greeted her once, it's enough. Oya come, have some more of my fruit. You know my bowl is too full. What about bread? Should I send the driver to buy fresh bread from the bakery?'

That useless witch had got me in trouble on my first morning home. I should have known that she would cause me all sorts of trouble because I had stood up to her, but this wasn't the time to dwell. I let it go as Dad cajoled and teased me until he chased my frown away.

'Okay,' I said, 'yes please.' Dad knew I loved that sweet bread from Madam Divine's bakery.

'Good girl,' he beamed approvingly, 'I like that smile much better.'

His smile faded a little as he looked up and said sharply 'Ebele, before doing anything else, please go outside and call me Edet. Karina wants Madam Divine's bread, and that's what she will have.'

'Dad, yes *sah*.' Instructions received, Ebele turned and left. I was going to enjoy being Dad's girl for a bit. Teacup now empty, Mum set her saucer down on the tray and smiled at us, 'Naiye, I can see you and your daughter are bonding over pawpaw, as usual. I'm going out to see a few people this morning and I'd like Ade to drive me. Will you be needing him for errands today?'

He returned her smile with a cheeky one of his own, 'No thank you, my dear. I'll drive myself today, but first I want to spend some time with this little madam over here. Let me hear a bit more about this Mr. Barido.' Sometimes I think Mum and Dad behave like teenagers, except she is more like the grown up.

This was the morning I needed. Dad and I talked, and he laughed at my stories and cracked my knuckles until Preye and Daniel joined us. Thank God I'd had my fruit before they descended on the bowl.

After lunch, Preye and I camped out in the larger area of the parlour, surrounded by sofas and armchairs. A plush carpet covered the terrazzo floor of the sitting area, and this was where we built our fort. I didn't know what a fort was, but it sounded cool because I heard it on films. The pouffes were our trees and the massive bean bag was the lake. This part of the parlour was the adults' area when we had guests, but the space made it perfect for our games. We played for hours at a time there, exploring every adventure that our imaginations could conjure up. It was here, in the middle of our game of "*ayo*" that Daniel found us. Or rather, where Daniel found me. I'd avoided him so far, knowing he wanted to know about the knife.

'Preye,' he called, 'there is ice cream in the kitchen for you.' Daniel knew how to trick Preye. He smirked at me as I watched the little traitor run off towards the kitchen with a happy squeal.

'Alright Karina,' flinging himself beside me, it he whispered urgently, 'spill. What's going on? What did that Ebele do to you? And have you found the knife?'

I shook my head. My heavy sigh mirrored my feelings about keeping secrets. Mum always said there should be no secrets among family, and there were almost none in our family. At least that's what I heard Mum say. We even knew that Uncle Pena had been caught with his neighbour's wife because the neighbour saw him sneaking away in the lady's bright purple Ankara blouse, which Uncle Pena had grabbed in his haste when he heard the husband's voice. Of course, no one ever let him forget it either. Nope. He was reminded at every turn, much to his chagrin.

We went for a walk then, my brother and me, so I could spill the terrible secret I'd hidden for so long. We said we were going to Domino Supermarket to buy ice cream. By the time we walked ourselves slowly back home, picking our way along the muddy, potholed road, Daniel knew most of it. I told him about playing hide and seek when Ebele hid with me in the kitchen and told me about sex between a man and a woman. And about my ninth birthday when she first came to my room at night, bringing her nasty body odour and onion smell with her, and how she slapped me when I tried to stop her roaming hands, saying it was my punishment for being disobedient to Mum. What I didn't say was that she took off her panties and sat on me. That was too disgusting. I only told him about how she looked at me.

Daniel said nothing for a long time after I finished speaking. Not a word. He walked silently for so long that I began to wonder if he would say anything at all.

We got all the way home and into his bedroom without him saying a single word. Had I said too much? Did he think I was lying? Would he tell Mum? Or worse, Ebele?

I looked around at his pale-grey-painted room with white furnishings like mine. As usual, it was a mess, with half his clothes lying on the floor, and his reading table littered with bits of paper covered in half drawn pictures in vivid colour. Mum would scold him if she came in here and saw the state of his room, I thought.

When the silence got too much to bear, I gnawed at my nails, already raw and bleeding from when I attacked them yesterday.

When finally he spoke, his words shocked me. 'Let's kill her.' He said it so quietly, I was sure I'd imagined it. 'We have to kill her Karina or report her to an adult who can deal with her.' The conviction in his fourteen-year-old voice made him sound like an adult.

'*Ehn*? What?!' I asked, so befuddled all I could do was croak at him, mouth agape. I thought for sure he had lost his mind. I probably had already lost mine when.

Daniel watched me closely. I worshipped my big brother, and even though he was tall and muscular, he was still a boy and just as powerless as I was.

I said nothing; what could I say? Hearing the words from his mouth made it so real. I was terrified, but I couldn't decide what terrified me more – the prospect of killing Ebele, or the fact that my brother suggested we kill her.

'Karina!'

The sound of my mum's voice jerked me from my reverie. Daniel and I exchanged looks. The woman sounded vexed!

I scrambled to get up. 'Oh God! What have I done now?' I put my hand to my forehead.

'KARINA!'

Mum was shouting, which was never a good sign. She never raised her voice. My bare feet pounded the floor as I searched for her. From Daniel's room through the small parlour, across the veranda and into the dining room, I skidded to a halt, my mouth wide open. Mum sat at the table, looking ready to slap somebody into the next week. Her fingers held a knife. My orange-handled knife. And that stupid Ebele stood next to her, sneering at me.

'Shit!' I thought. And as incongruous as it seemed, my mind spent a half second on the fact that I had now become a person who swore. *Chei*! Uncle Akpan would be disappointed in me if he found out, and I quickly breathed a prayer 'God please don't be angry.'

With my accusers waiting for an answer to a question I was yet to be asked, I wondered what on earth I would say. Could I craft the right story? Would they believe me? Elders were never wrong, but children usually were. Before I could say a word, Mum spoke, her voice low and controlled now.

'Karina, I'm going to ask you this question exactly once,' she said in that voice that almost made me wet myself. 'What was this knife doing under your pillow?'

My brain and mouth disconnected. I looked up at the witch and quickly looked back down. So, she had taken my knife when I was sleeping. I knew I should point the finger at her and tell my Mum what she had been doing to me, but my brain had gone blank. No wonder she called me a *fear-fear* chicken.

'Answer me, Karina,' Mum was tiring of waiting for me, so I did the only thing I could think of. I lied. Well, I meant to lie. But as I opened my mouth to say, 'it wasn't me,' the lump that had been hiding in my throat all morning began breaking into small pieces.

My gaze fixed on my mother. She, my warrior mother, my protector, had become my inquisitor. Why didn't she know that the two-faced demon behind her was my tormentor? Why didn't she know that it exhausted me, being afraid all the time? Her eyes narrowed. If I could produce a bit of drama, maybe I could buy myself some time. If I was reporting Ebele, it wouldn't be in front of her, so with a sob, I collapsed on the cool, marble floor. Mum, alarmed and confused, picked me up and stood there just holding me, rocking us both back and forth. How long I stood in her embrace, I'll never know. Eventually her hand rubbed circles on my back, soothing me like my protector again. Her voice pitched so low, only my ears could hear her say, 'Enough now, my darling. Don't cry anymore,' over and over like a mantra. The familiar, comforting smell of her made me feel better for a time, and when my tears gave way to hiccups, she walked us from the dining room to the parlour and sat me down on a sofa.

I looked up to see Mum waiting - patient but expectant – and I sighed. I would have to tell her the truth.

'What's the matter, my darling girl?' Mum asked, the crossness in her voice replaced by concern. I never cried like that. 'What happened, Karina? Why did you have a knife? You can tell me anything, don't be afraid.'

Maybe it was time to tell someone who could *do* something about it. I had been twisting the hem of my dress around my fingers, my other nervous habit. Hoping to summon some extra courage, my eyes wandered to the hallway to see if Daniel was standing by, ready to help and encourage. The hallway stood empty. Still, it was time. Looking cautiously up and took a deep breath. 'I took it to protect myself,' my voice was hoarse.

I studied her closely. Just as I expected, her eyebrows shot up, causing her forehead to wrinkle in confusion, 'I don't understand. Protect yourself from what? From whom? In this house?!' Her head swivelled from side to side as her voice intensified, looking suspiciously like she hoped to find the culprit hiding behind the curtains or some such place.

'Mum…' I placed my hand on hers to draw her attention, first checking to make sure we were alone and could not be heard. But before another word came out, the door opened and Ebele poked her ugly head in the room.

Her eyes swept over me, 'Madam,' addressing my mum, '*I say make I come check on Karina. This one wey she dey cry like say person die so, I hope say no problem.*' Ebele looked appropriately concerned.

In a single breath, I lost my moment of truth. Why did she have to show up now? What if she was right and Mum didn't believe me? Grownups don't believe children, they believe other grownups. 'She's fine, thank you Ebele. Please excuse us, we haven't finished talking.'

'Yes, ma. Sorry, Ma.'

Mum turned back to me. 'You were saying?'

'I'm sorry, Mum. In school, one of the girls said she would beat me up me for telling the prefect she stole some meat from the tureen during lunch one day. She and another girl came at after lights out and dragged me out of bed. If Senior Juliet hadn't woken up, they would have beaten me up. I was afraid, so I started to take a knife with me to bed at night to protect myself. It's just become a habit.' I was getting so good at lying.

Mum looked sceptical, leaning back and squinting at me suspiciously. I could tell she didn't really believe my story, but I had told it. I couldn't change it. I would say no more, despite her prodding. 'Okay,' she sighed, 'I have to talk to your teacher. One girl cannot be frightening you this way. I will come with you when school resumes and speak to your House Mistress about this.'

She pulled me close while making shushing noises. 'Enough now,' she said, 'stop crying and wash your face. And please don't take a knife with you to bed again.'

As I got up to leave, I noticed that Ebele had crept back in. She smirked at me, and I scowled at her. She may have won this round, but I wouldn't give up.

The rest of the evening passed in a blur, and my mind ran a thousand directions. How crazy was Daniel's foolish pronouncement? How could we kill Ebele? How would we go about such a thing? I had already tried, failed, and almost got caught. But what would happen if we did nothing? Ebele was the adult, and she outsmarted me. My short-lived defiance had been put down. But what if she started "playing" with Preye who could not fend for herself?

That night, sleep eluded me. My thoughts obsessed over what my brother had said. My ears heard the pipes that signalled the start of the nine o'clock news. John Momoh droned on with the news in Pidgin English, then in English. My body, wrapped in my tiger nightie, tossed and turned until the house fell silent, and I prayed with all my might that she wouldn't come to me. A deep, gnawing ache arose in my belly.

#

Dear Diary,

After mummy showed me the knife, I couldn't sleep. Not even after the news was done. My tummy was hurting me again – Ebele was angry, and I was afraid of what she might do to me. I think God was listening to me that night, because she didn't come to my room after all. I heard Daddy go to bed and waited until mummy came out to the parlour to pray before I fell asleep. When I woke up the next morning, Daniel was calling me to eat breakfast. We were having fried plantain and eggs. I said no thank you and he was really surprised. I was sure I would vomit if I ate anything.

The next day, Daniel moved in with me and Preye for the night and we camped out on a mattress on the floor. We took some food to bed with us so that we could pretend to be like the children I read about in Enid Blyton's books, with their midnight feasts. We didn't have 'lashings of lemonade' or anything else, but we were happy with plantain chips, slices of bread with thick layers of margarine, ground nuts, and sweets. We drank Ribena because mummy won't let us have Coca Cola.

Once Preye was asleep, Daniel and I lay down on the mattress in the middle of my bedroom and talked in hushed tones about Ebele. About killing and how that was bad. And how maybe it could be good since she was bad. I told him about the pain in my tummy when I thought of Ebele and what if I was dying. Then he told me about his school and the girl he liked, and we laughed until mummy shouted at us to go to sleep.

Daniel and I have a secret that doesn't include Preye and we used to always tell each other everything, even though she's little. Now when we play 'The Three Musketeers' *we won't mean it because we broke our promise to never keep secrets. We're just trying to protect her though. I don't want her to know about Ebele and her games.*

****

At Sunday School, we sang Sister Caro's favourite chorus. I'm sure she likes it because it's more like a test than a song of praise. We have to regurgitate the memory verses that she gives us each week.

God has something to say, God has something to say,

Listen, listen, Pay much attention

For God has something to say!'

At this point in the song, we all had to wait and see which unlucky person Sister Caro's crooked finger of judgement would point to.

I furiously scrambled around in my brain to find a memory verse to recite, but she chose the girl who was sitting beside me instead. I was happy because I couldn't remember anything.

The girl got up and recited the only memory verse most of us could ever remember, 'John three sixteen: For God so loved the world that He gave His only begotten son that whosoever believes in him should not perish but have everlasting life…' The rest of us sighed, relieved to have dodged a bullet.

CHAPTER ELEVEN

The long holidays went quickly and before we knew it, four weeks of the six-week break had passed. Me and Dan spent most of our time together, whispering about different things and playing with our friends who lived on our street. We rode our Chopper bicycles, climbed trees, and built forts with Preye. I turned twelve, but we didn't have a party. Instead Mum took Kaine, Dan, Preye and I to Mr. Bigg's fast foods to buy meat-pies and ice-cream.

One evening, after Kaine had gone home, me and Dan were whispering about how Ebele no longer came to my room. She was there, always looking angry, but she didn't come to me. 'I don't know how long it will last, Daniel,' I said, 'Ebele is really a bitch and I don't know what she will do.'

'Who is a witch?' Preye piped up, completely mishearing. Oh God. I didn't know she could hear us.

'What?' Daniel looked as concerned as I felt. Mum would kill us if she heard Preye say that about Ebele.

'You said Ebele is a witch. Is she really a witch? Does she fly on a broomstick at night when everybody is sleeping?' Her eyes were like saucers.

'Erm, no no… we, erm, we weren't talking about Ebele. We were talking about Osita's new bike,' Daniel answered guiltily.

'It's a lie, you were talking about Ebele. I heard you.' She pointed at me, 'Karina said so, and now you're saying it was Osita's bike. Is his bike called Ebele?' Hands planted on her hips, she looked accusingly at us.

'Would we lie to you, Preye? You know we don't keep secrets. If it was Ebele, we would have told you. I'm sure your ears are dirty again. *Oya* come, let's go and get some ice-cream and then you have to clean your ears.' She allowed herself to be appeased by my offer and stopped asking questions. We went off together and I thanked God that she had let the matter drop.

The following week, I had a sleep-over at Kaine's house. I hadn't spent very much time with her, so I asked Mum and she let the driver drop me off. Me and Kaine sat in her bedroom, gossiping and giggling about our first year in secondary school and the boys from Stella Maris Comprehensive who come to our schools to chase girls. Kaine's school was Federal Government Girls' School, Abuloma, which was a much better school than Livingstone. We whispered about what it was like to wear a bra and to have our periods. We would soon be teenagers!

She told me of the senior student in her school who got pregnant, and how their principal called the girl out during Assembly and told the entire school that she was a disgrace to be pregnant at her age and not married. Then the principal told everybody to shame her. I knew what she meant because we did it in my school too. The principal would say 'Shame,

shame, shame,' and we would all would point at the poor girl standing in front, and shout 'shame' at her. I knew a girl who didn't cry when we shamed her. The Principal said she was a bad girl without home training. The girl did not cry when she was beaten with a '*koboko*' – a bendy bamboo whip. Not even when some students said, 'the blood of Jesus,' while crossing their arms over the breasts they wish they had. Maybe she was tired of feeling ashamed. Or maybe she knew that crying wouldn't change anything. Kaine said the girl in her school cried though.

I said, '*Chei*, poor girl,' but Kaine shushed me, putting her hand over my mouth and peering at the door. She said I shouldn't let her mum hear me feeling sorry for a bad girl.

I asked how the girl got pregnant. Kaine said she had been holding hands with one boy from Stella Maris Boys' School. I heard that when you start having your periods, touching a boy can make you pregnant, and I told Kaine.

'*Tufiakwa*! God forbid!' Kaine and I clicked our fingers over our heads to ward off bad luck. We agreed to never hold hands with any boys.

I fell silent then, thinking how horrible it would have been to stand in front of all those people, having them shame you for something that happened to you. What if that had been me? If anyone ever found out about the thing that happened, would they shame me the same way? Maybe they would stop speaking to me, like Kaine said they did to the girl who was pregnant. People don't like to be near you when bad things happen. I'm not sure exactly why.

We filled the last week with school activities – Mum taking us to be measured for our new uniforms, before going to 'Town' market to buy our school shoes for the term. We bought provisions for me to take to boarding school, along with books, pencils, pens and math sets. Daniel was a day student, so he didn't need as many things as I did. I knew that I would miss home, but I was a little pleased to be escaping the constant shadow that Ebele cast over everything.

CHAPTER TWELVE

Daniel had written me a letter. He sent it with Mum and Ade when they came to see me on visiting day and brought the usual provisions and Mum's delicious fried rice with chicken. Sometimes we ate the chicken together, other times she would say she was on a diet which made me laugh. Mums should be squishy.

I enjoyed visiting days because it was just Mum and I (and sometimes Preye) for a few precious minutes, and we laughed and prattled about anything while I devoured whatever cooked food she had brought. At home I had to share her with everyone else, so this alone time became precious.

Some visits lasted more than an hour, which was always great, but that visit ended too early. Just before visiting time ended, she shared the most unexpected news. Ebele had left us.

My greasy fingers were holding the last piece of spicy chicken when she said it. My head jerked up to search her face for a moment before looking back down. 'Good. Let her go,' I said this so quietly, I couldn't tell whether she heard me. I didn't ask where Ebele had gone, and I couldn't care less as long as she was gone. Without fanfare, I wiped my greasy fingers on the tissue Mum handed me and held out my hands to show her my nails.

'Mum, see. I have stopped biting my fingernails.' Perhaps if I focused on something else, my heart would stop hammering away so loudly. Mum didn't say anything for several long seconds. Then she moved on with me and told me well done for kicking the habit of a lifetime.

When our time together ended, she hugged me so tight and for so long that I thought I would stop breathing. 'Right my darling, it's time for me to go,' she said when she released me, 'be good and take care of yourself, baby girl.' She handed me the bag of provisions and busied herself with kicking me out of the car where we had been sitting. 'Love you!' Her eyes glistened with what looked suspiciously like tears, but I said nothing. After all, I always shed a few tears whenever visiting was over.

The heels of my sandals dragged in the dust on the way back to my dorm. All I could manage was a half-hearted greeting to Ma'Sei as I passed her sitting in front of the gate to the quadrangle. I put my provisions in my locker. Daniel's letter sat in the bag's top, so I put it in my pocket and went to hide away in Senior Julie's room to read my letter.

He said Ebele had been the centre of drama again. Only this time it was not somebody's husband she had gone for; it was a family that lived across the street from us - The Ugochis. Ebele was looking after their daughter and Preye while the neighbour went to the market. The girl said that Ebele called her to come and collect some sweets from her in her room, and on pretext of looking at her new underwear had touched her in her special place. The neighbour found out later that evening when she was giving her daughter a bath because the child was crying about her fanny hurting her. She told her mum that Ebele put something in there. The neighbour had marched straight to our house, told Mum, and they both confronted the bitch. Daniel said she confessed, but only after Mum had given her a hot slap or two for talking nonsense to the lady. Daniel said that Ebele was stunned and stammered her excuses. Maybe she didn't expect anyone to report her, because I didn't. Naturally, she blamed the devil for her behaviour. I rolled my eyes when I read that… Poor Satan.

Trembling fingers folded the letter carefully into the envelope as salty tears charged down my face yet again. One landed on the envelope, like a period marking the end of the chapter. Should I thank God for exposing her as the predator she was? Or be ashamed that it wasn't me who exposed her like I should have? Maybe I could have kept that other girl safe. Relief and shame washed over me. I wondered how long it would be before someone asked me if she had ever tried to touch me and Preye the same way; and if she did, why I never told my mum. Did Mum suspect something? The way she looked at me made me think so. My thoughts raced through a dozen answers to the inevitable questions, but I remained scared. No response I could think of seemed good enough. But why did I remain scared? It wasn't like Ebele could do anything to me now that she was gone, but still the fear lingered. And it was different now.

Now I feared that everybody would look at me differently. That they would ask me 'why didn't you tell anybody?' And then I would be in trouble. Maybe they would think that I liked what Ebele did, although I really didn't. In my innermost heart, I think what I was most scared of was that even though Ebele had gone, my mind wouldn't be able to escape her wickedness and smelly body.

'God,' I whispered, 'please let nobody ask me anything about Ebele, because if they ask me, I will lie, and I know you don't like people that lie. If you help me, I promise not to laugh at Sister Felicia when she's running away from the dog, I will stop asking so many questions, I will remember my memory verses from church.' I prayed and prayed, but God must have been sleeping again when I talked to him.

#

When next I was home, Aunty Emi brought Kaine to our house for a visit. 'Aunty Emi!' I screamed as I launched myself into her open arms.

'Oh, my baby! You're back from school! And growing like a weed this year!' She wrapped me up in her soft arms and familiar scent, pulling me to her ample chest in a warm embrace.

'Good afternoon Aunty,' my face felt like it would split from smiling so wide. Aunty Emi was my favourite aunt. She was more fun than all my other aunties and always had butter mints in her handbag. I never met anyone who could resist her smile.

'Karina, Karina! How are you, my dear?' She beamed back at me. Aunty Emi always smelled like a curious mix of gardenias and cocoa butter. Her body and soul were soft and cuddly, and she seemed to forever be smiling.

Aunty Emi was so different from my Mum who was the older sister by a few years. She boldly wore her hair short and curly, her skin glowed smooth and dark. She prayed all the time, talked *a lot*, and no subject was a taboo. My mum had light skin and long, permed hair had a slimmer body that still felt soft when she hugged me. Mum wore light makeup and Estee Lauder's 'Beautiful' perfume all the time, and spoke like she only had a limited number of words to use each day. She could paralyse a person with one look or a carefully placed word. Mum wore flowing kaftans and *boubous*, while Aunty Emi was almost always in a blouse and wrapper. She never wore makeup, but she was beautiful anyway. No matter how different they were, Mum and Aunty Emi were extremely close and fiercely protective of their families.

'I'm fine, thank you. Aunty where is Kaine?'

'She's coming. She's just greeting your Dad.' She peered into my face, 'I hope that silly Ebele didn't try anything funny with you while she was here, Karina. Because I told your mum that someone like that woman, she could have done and undone without being caught. She should never have been trusted. I told your mum I didn't trust her!'

My smile faded away before I mumbled something under my breath about going to find Kaine and made my escape. My excitement at seeing Kaine had dulled because of the questions I knew were coming next. Daniel, Kaine, Preye and I played outside, and Daniel's friend from down the street came to ask if we wanted to ride our bicycles with him. I wasn't interested.

Later, busy hands cleared away the empty dishes and mostly empty bowls of boiled yams and delicious fish stew. Aunty Emi clicked on the TV and everyone hurried to grab a seat in the sitting room. Well, almost everyone. Mum and Dad stayed at the dining table. The sound of my name rang through the house.

'Karina!'

Dad was the one who called me, but I pretended not to hear him because I was talking to Daniel. 'Karina!' He called me again, and this time Daniel nudged me.

'Daddy is calling you.'

'Yes, Dad?' I dragged myself to the dining room, suddenly angry. What was the matter with me?

'Sit down, my daughter,' he gestured to a chair between him and Mum. 'Your mother and I want to talk to you.'

I sat down and studied the pattern of circles on the tablecloth. I took a deep breath and clenched my jaw.

'Karina,' Mum lifted my chin to make me look up at her, 'honey, I'm sure you know by now why Ebele left this house. We sent her away because Mrs Ugochi's daughter from next door said Ebele was touching her private place.' She stopped to clear her throat as if there was something stuck there, but she didn't let go of my face. 'Karina, your Dad and I have to ask you this question. Did Ebele fiddle with you like that?'

I didn't speak for a few seconds. 'Fiddle with me in what way?'

She shot a look at Dad 'like how she touched Mrs Ugochi's daughter. Did she touch you like that?

You know you can tell us, and we won't be mad at you.'

Why was I so angry? I wanted to shout at them, but I didn't. I thought of the last time Mum scolded me for waking up late and how she looked at my underwear on the floor in disgust. Why didn't she ask me what my panties were doing on the floor, knowing well that I always slept in my underwear and my nightie? Now what was I going to say?

Mum thinks that when people don't look you in the face, it means they're lying. I lifted my eyes to hers, feeling defiant, 'and if she did *fiddle* with me Mum, what will you do? She has left this house and you won't bring her back.' Was it my imagination, or was her left eye twitching?

'Karina! There's no need for that.' She was taken aback, and I was strangely satisfied.

'We just want to know so we can help you, Karina. We're your parents and we love you, so there's no need to talk to your Mum like that.' Dad's hand drifted to cover hers and give it a gentle squeeze. Why was he comforting her? Why did she look so scared?

I shook my head and sighed. 'I'm sorry Mum, I don't know what happened. No, she didn't do anything to me.'

She narrowed her eyes and looked at me as if to see into my soul for the truth. 'Are you sure?'

'Yes mum, I'm sure.'

Relief washed across her face in a flash. She looked at Dad, then back at me and smiled. 'Thank God!' she whispered forcefully as she patted my cheek and blinked rapidly. 'Okay you can go.'

I looked sideways at her when I stood up. How could she not see? My feet felt like ten-pound weights as I crossed the kitchen floor, thinking what a good actor I was. I didn't notice that I was biting a fingernail again, or that Dad was watching me thoughtfully as I slowly trudged out of sight.

#

Dear Diary,

When I lied to Mum that Ebele hadn't handled me, I thought she must have seen right through me and into my dirty little secret; I was not a good little girl anymore. I was a bad girl because I let the bitch touch me in my special place and I didn't tell anybody.

Maybe she had been right when she said I liked it really, although I know that I hated it. I hate that she took away my power; she took away my laugh and she made me afraid. I hated that she had made me sin, and now God wouldn't want me anymore. I had no choice but to keep on sinning, and of course, I would go to hell. I didn't want to go to hell. Brother Akpan had described it as hot and smelly and scary. He said that there would be maggots everywhere, and that no matter how much people cried and begged and were in pain, they would never stop being tormented.

Ebele told me that God would not forgive me. It confused me a lot because that wasn't what I learned in church. I told her that in church we learned that God would always forgive our sins. She said it was true that God would forgive some sins, but that he wouldn't forgive little girls who did sex with adults.

Don't tell anybody, but what she said made me think two things: First was that God is confusing. My name, Ayebakarinateh, means God has answered my prayers. Dad says the good Lord may not come when you call him, but he's always on time… Well, I think that He takes too long to answer me, and He has never been on time for me. Second is that I'm not sure what sex is, but I know that it's a bad thing. I wonder if it is the sort of wrestling Ebele and her friends play.

It's so strange going to bed without worrying about Ebele. The first night, when the jingle of the nine o'clock news on NTA started, I went to bed, but I couldn't sleep. I thought I would be able to sleep, but that changed after I smelled her. Maybe it was my mind.

Do you know that in foreign countries like England, when the king dies, they say 'the king is dead, long live the king'? I thought that was strange, but Dad said they're just welcoming the new king. When I was coming home from school in the car with Ade, I remembered and repeated it to myself, 'The bitch is dead, long live the bitch.'

It made me laugh a little, even though there was nothing funny. Ebele is gone. Not dead gone, just gone from our home. I am glad, but I'm still scared. No, not scared. Nervous. And I'm angry, and I don't even know who I'm angry with – Ebele or Mum. And Dad, but only a little bit. Mum should have known, shouldn't she? Now she and Dad think I will come and tell them something. Well, I won't!

CHAPTER THIRTEEN

Karina, 1998

The cool, dry winds of the harmattan period made January my favourite time of the year. After the Christmas and New Year celebrations, we barely had time to stop before Mum was back to buying the provisions that signalled that it was nearly time to return to school. By this time, it almost seemed like Ebele had never existed. Nobody really spoke of her, yet she didn't stop appearing in my dreams, suffocating me with her unpleasantness.

I read a book where a girl made her wicked stepfather disappear by forgetting him. She had decided to pretend he didn't exist, as though she could no longer hear his voice or see him. When he spoke, she refused to hear. When he walked past her, she pretended not to see him. She didn't mention his name or address him, and even when he smacked her, she didn't cry out, no matter how painful it was. In the story, the more she pretended, the more faded he became. She pretended until he began to fade away like a pencil drawing that was being erased a little at a time, until he was gone.

I knew it was only a story, but maybe I could do it too. Maybe I could force her out of my mind, along with her persistent smell of stale onions and body odour that assaulted my nostrils when she was near. I would forget the smirk on her stupid face and her foul breath, and just maybe if I succeeded, the things she did to me would also go away. My willpower resolved to try. I may not have been able to kill her, but somehow, I would make the witch cease to exist.

I didn't know how to behave, now that Ebele wasn't around. I wasn't unhappy, just angry. I laughed, but it felt hollow. At church last Sunday, we sang '*God has something to say…*' I didn't sing with the other children. And when Sister Caro called me to say my memory verse, I simply said I didn't know any verses. It didn't matter to me if that was rude or that she knew I lied in church.

When we got home, Dad said there would be a family meeting after lunch. Daniel rolled his eyes '*Ach*. This man and his family meetings. Why can't he just talk to us like normal people, instead of waiting until the end of every school holiday? I want to watch my tv program this afternoon!' I didn't have the time to tell him that Dad was standing behind him.

'So, your television program is more important than talking with your family, is it? Tell me, those who wrote that show, do they live here?'

Dan gulped. 'No Dad, I didn't mean it like that…' If we were white people, his face would have been red.

Dad's large hand went up, stopping the flow of Dan's jabbering, 'Son, stop talking before you say things you shouldn't. Our family meetings are for us to discuss whatever is on our minds. It's our "safe space" where we can say anything we like with 'no judgement' whatever that means. You can use it or leave it, but I have something to tell you all without you jumping down my throat, so even though you may not want or need the meeting space, I do.'

Looking suitably chastised, Dan said, 'Sorry, Dad.'

But Dad had turned his attention to his newspaper and simply pointed at the door without looking up. That meant we had to clear off and fast.

After lunch, we cleared the table and then sat down around the parlour. Dad didn't smile. He cleared his throat and began, but didn't say his usual speech about how we needed to work hard at school. Instead, he said, 'You all know that I've been travelling to Lagos quite a bit recently. That's because I've been transferred. I've had a promotion at work and my office will be based in Lagos, so your Mum and I have agreed that we should move the family as soon as possible.'

Dan and I looked at each other and then at Mum. 'Lagos? Who do we know in Lagos? What about school and our friends?' He didn't look thrilled at the announcement, and I didn't know how I felt.

'Yes, Daniel - Lagos. And we will make new friends, don't worry.' Mum's tone was reassuring, and she rubbed his back.

Dad said his recent trips to Lagos had been to find us a new house, and we would live in a place called Ikoyi. He said it would be exciting, and we were to think of it like one of those adventures we read about in our Enid Blyton books. It would be a fresh start and as we would be moving soon, Daniel and I won't be going back to school in the new term. A new school and new friends would be waiting when we got to Lagos.

'Wait, but that means we won't be able to say goodbye to our friends,' I did know how I felt about this announcement. Not happy. 'What about Kaine? And Affie?'

'You will see Kaine during holidays, sweetheart. You will visit each other during the school holidays.' That didn't help the sinking feeling in my tummy, but she had moved on to Preye, who was clamouring for attention.

Preye was excited because Mum told her she can have her own room and choose the colour to paint it. Of course, she shouted 'Purple!' and we laughed. No surprises there.

It was nearly five o'clock when Mum sent me and Daniel out to buy groundnuts from Mama Charlie. As we traversed the long path, he blabbered away about a film he watched with his friend, Osita, but my ears weren't listening. I didn't know when he finished talking, nor did I hear the question he had asked me. Daniel nudged me with his elbow.

'Karina, what is the matter? I thought that now that the bitch has left us, you would be happy. But you are not happy. Throughout this holiday you've been quieter than before, and you don't laugh and play with me and Preye anymore. You're not eating any ice cream or chocolate, not even your favourite plantain and eggs.'

I shrugged nonchalantly. 'Dude, what do you want me to say? I have nothing to say, Dan. I'm okay.'

'Karina, please. Please tell me what's the matter. Didn't you already tell me the worst thing? Why are you not happy?'

He kicked at a stone on the path, which drew my attention to his spindly legs. He was getting taller. I looked up at his face, but he was busy examining his toes.

I felt sorry for him. He sounded confused, but what could I say? I couldn't explain myself.

'Daniel, I don't know what the matter is, and that's the truth. I just don't have anything to say and I don't feel like being happy. Ebele has left but I am still afraid that she will come back. I'm confused and when I think of her, it makes my tummy hurt and I don't know why. I told Mum and Dad that she didn't do anything to me, but what if they find out I was lying?'

He was looking at me now and his face looked just as hopeless as I felt. He reached out and held my hand as we carried on walking. 'Don't be afraid Karina, it will be okay.'

'But how?' I asked.

'I don't know, but it will,' he squeezed my hand. 'See, Mama Charlie has just made a fresh batch of groundnuts,' he pointed at her as she peeled the skin off the groundnuts she had just roasted and was preparing to bag.

'Good afternoon ma, *we come buy groundnut*,' as if we could possibly be trying to buy anything else at a place that sold only groundnuts.

'Thank you, my children, *how una dey*?' She asked, enquiring after our wellbeing, '*What of una mama and papa?*'

Our mouths watered as we politely answered her enquiries about our parents. She nodded then greeted the other customers as they waited for her to finish our order. She quickly stuffed a handful of free nuts in a paper cone for our walk home, handing it to us with our purchase and insisting, '*make una chop this one reach house.*' We thanked her and made our way home. I teased Daniel that it was because she could see him trying to consume her groundnuts through his nostrils.

As we walked, I thought of all the things I would miss when we moved to Lagos… Walking with Daniel to buy treats; Mama Charlie and her loud greetings; my bedroom and the way the terrazzo floor felt under my feet on a warm day, not to mention the whole compound and the sounds of the house as it woke up and when it was asleep. I would miss Mallam Bukio and Edet, and perhaps more, I would miss Ade and his funny accent. Mum said Kaine would visit often, but it won't be the same. Kaine and Affie are who I would miss most of all.

#

Dear Diary,

This evening Dad was talking to Uncle Eddie and said how it is important to always tell the truth and not keep secrets from your family. He said secrets can kill a person. I can't imagine how any secret can come out of your mind to kill you. Will it stab you? Or poison you? Then I thought, maybe secrets are those voices in your head that torment you when no one else can hear. Like my secret…

God, can you read? If you can, then you should know that I'm not talking to you anymore because I'm angry with you.

Yes, I said it. I don't really like Lagos, and I thought you knew that. How come you don't ever give me things I like? Why are we not moving to a nice place like London instead? When we went to Lagos to get our visas for London, I hated it because the place was crowded with big yellow molue buses, cars and people, and everybody seemed to speak in Yoruba. I didn't understand when the woman who was plaiting my hair spoke to me, so she knocked my head with the comb.

****

Dear Diary,

Welcome to Lagos. We now live in a big estate in Ikoyi, which is a very nice part of Lagos where there's not so much shouting. There are masses of plants everywhere, with pink and orange bougainvillea decorating the fences, dwarf palms growing along the boundary between the lawn and paved driveway, and gardenia bushes with their dark green leaves and fragrant white blooms mixed in with other flowers in beds and pots to create a jungle where we can get lost when we choose. Preye and I played hide and seek in the 'jungle' and it was fun.

It feels strange being in a new house. We each have our own bedrooms upstairs, and Peshe has her bedroom downstairs near the kitchen. School will resume in two weeks' time, so the three of us spend the time riding our bikes and learning some new dance steps. We have a mango tree in the compound, so we climb it to pluck mangoes sometimes. Dad took us swimming in Ikoyi club yesterday, and Preye nearly swallowed the pool. She still doesn't swim well, but she refused to let anybody help her. Silly girl. Dad didn't beat her for being silly and almost drowning, but I thought he should have done that instead of buying her coke and gala sausage roll.

I dreamt about the bitch yesterday, Diary. She had no hands in my dream, so when she tried to pinch me, she could not. I think that forgetting her is working, so maybe when next she forces herself into my mind or my dreams, she would have no smell and another part of her would be missing. Maybe her face, then her legs, then the rest of her. A person with no hands to do anything does not scare me. I told Mum that I had a bad dream. She said I should start exercising with her because it would help me sleep better. Mum goes running with the lady next door. I know she's not the same age as my Mum, because she calls her 'Aunty', but Mum doesn't seem to mind having her around. They wear matching t-shirts and shorts when they go running and I think they look nice. Mum said they run around the park in the middle of the estate. I think I will go with them tomorrow morning, but I won't wear the same colour t-shirt as them.

PART TWO

CHAPTER FOURTEEN

Karina, 2017

The rush of words tumbles and falls until I finally run out. Then the roar of silence is deafening. Akin is so still it's almost unnerving. The only thing that betrays his emotion is the bobbing of his Adam's apple.

I've told him about how it felt to be under Ebele's spell, needing to be approved by her, even while I hated her. The confusion I felt at the start and the self-loathing that followed every day after. I explained the reason for my aversion to onions and hide-and-seek.

'I need to feel safe, Akin… and I don't feel safe with Tosan,' I blurt out, surprising us both.

We are sitting side by side, my left hand held loosely between Akin's large hands. As always, I'm dwarfed by the sheer size of him. We've been sitting now for over an hour, looking out at the field while I talked. A few times, my voice drifted into long silences, but he gave me the space I needed to tell the story on my own terms. Apart from asking a few questions here and there for clarification, he's been silent, but the different emotions I catch chasing across his face each time I look up tell me that he has many more questions. Part of me knows that he'll wait until I'm ready and able to hear them.

'I'm just not sure anymore, Akin,' I say, shaking my head, partly in wonder and partly to buttress my point. I'm a little surprised by the words that are coming out of my mouth. When did I arrive at this decision or not-decision?

Lost in my own thoughts, it eventually dawns on me that Akin is saying something. He looks confused.

'Erm, I don't understand, Karina. What you've just told me is one thing, and it's huge to be dealing with today. I mean, you've told me bits of it before, but I didn't know all of it. I certainly didn't know you threatened to kill her! But what has this all got to do with Tosan? What did he do wrong?'

'That's the confusing part. It's not what he's done, Akin. It's me and the fact that I've been unsettled for a while now. Perhaps a bit late, but I've come to realise that I don't even know what I want. Am I marrying him because I love him or because it's expected of me?'

The first time Tosan met my Dad, it was quickly established that he was the eldest son of Dad's business partner, Chief Yeka James. When our parents found out we were dating, questions and insinuations about marriage followed swiftly, and there was no going back. Or was there?

I shake my head. 'Tosan hasn't got anything to do with Ebele. The past is gone, and I clearly still have some issues with it, but I'm not saying the two are related. Or maybe they are, like one affected the other somehow. No matter how hard I try, Akin, my imagination cannot invoke a forever with Tosan. Sure, I can see the wedding, our three children, nice house, etc. But when I think about the everydayness of us, my heart just fills with dread and that's God's truth.'

Akin looks even more perplexed now, if that is possible, and I almost feel sorry for him.

'Dude, stop looking at me like I'm crazy and say something.'

'Like what?!'

'I don't know. Anything. We're running out of time, and Mum is going to send out a search party anytime now, if she hasn't already.' I look down at my watch to check the time. It's nearly eleven o'clock - six hours to go.

He cocks his head to the left in scepticism, 'You're here telling me that you don't want to get married, but you're concerned about when the wedding is starting?' He sighs. 'Okay, let's strip it back, and then I'm taking you home to your mum. Whatever happens next, I think you need to talk all this through with Aunty and Uncle. I'm assuming you haven't told them of your doubts?'

'They don't know, Akin, you're the first person I've told. I hadn't really admitted it to myself either,' I respond a little sheepishly. The truth is that Mum has been asking me for months what the matter was, commenting that I wasn't as excited as she would have expected a bride to be. When we were discussing the flower choices for the bridal bouquet a couple of months ago, she came straight out and asked me. I'd passed on yet another decision during the consultation with the wedding planner – the choice of cake flavours, place settings, décor, and then my bouquet. As we got in the car to head back home, I started talking about the ideas I had for a new commission I'd just taken on. My interior design business was beginning to take off, and a trip or two to South Africa or Marrakech were in order before the wedding. She turned to look at me.

'Karina what's going on with you? Is all well?'

I paused mid-sentence, 'erm … yes, why wouldn't it be?'

'Well, for one thing you're clearly more excited about decorating someone's house than your upcoming marriage. You didn't give Mrs Uche any clear direction about your flowers. Instead, I ended up choosing the flowers for your own bouquet.'

'*Haba* Mum,' I interrupted her, 'you know more about flowers than I ever could! Why on earth should I get in the middle of that? It's not that big of a deal.'

'Okay, let's say I buy that. What would you say about when we chose the décor for the church and reception hall? Or the cake tasting? You might as well not have been there because Preye and I ended up deciding for you while you simply agreed with whatever was said. I've seen more enthusiasm from a potted plant, Karina!'

Her exasperation was clear to see.

'Mum, I don't know what you're talking about,' I played innocent, although I knew precisely what she was talking about. 'It's only one day, this wedding. Aren't you the one who's always saying how there's more to marriage than the big day?' I thought parroting her words would distract her.

'Don't do that, baby girl. Don't pretend you don't know what I mean. You're not really excited about planning your wedding,' she took my hand between hers, dropping her voice even lower. 'Has something happened between you and Tosan? If he is misbehaving, you should tell me now so that we can deal with it before the wedding day.'

I rolled her words around my head a little and got curious. 'So, if he has "messed up"' I added some air quotes for emphasis, 'who is "we" and how will you deal with it?'

Her response was swift and sure. 'Is he not a man? Men can be a bit silly sometimes! Your father and I can talk to him so he can make amends quickly. It's too early for him to be messing about.'

Not sure why I found that response so disappointing, but lips forced a smile 'No Mum, I'm good. I guess I'm over the wedding day hype and just want it to be here already. I'll try to be a bit more enthusiastic.' And I did try, until today.

'Karina,' Akin's voice pulls me back to him, 'Do your mum and dad know any of the other things you've told me or even left out this morning?'

'They know some stuff. We don't talk about this shit, remember? Please Akin, let's just focus on today. I can only deal with one big reveal at a time.'

'But shouldn't you tell them?'

'I don't want them to worry unnecessarily. And in my defence, I wasn't entirely sure how I felt about the wedding until just now.'

'Fair enough. See, I know how you process things, but now that you've said it, you can't take it back. You must tell them. Even if it's just to work through how you're feeling *before* the wedding.' His gaze is stern; his voice insistent as he grips my arm, gently shaking me to communicate the urgency of what he is saying.

'I've heard you. I will tell them. Or maybe I should tell Mum first?' My heart thuds in response as I swallow hard. The enormity of my musings and what I had just committed to tell my folks were huge. A heavy sigh pushes me over the edge. 'I guess I'd better go home and let the chips fall where they may. I don't know what we will end up deciding, but you must promise me you won't tell a soul what I told you *until* I say so. Not even Tosan.'

'Of course.'

'Say you promise, Akin,' I insist a little childishly. Akin's smile is a little sad as he gets up off the grass and stretches out his hand to pull me to my feet, 'I promise. Now I have a lot of questions, but the first thing to do is get you home so we can sort things out with Uncle and Aunty. If there is to be no wedding today, I don't even want to imagine the *wahala* that will unfold.'

'Well, there will be drama one way or other for sure, but I reckon trouble before the wedding will be better than waiting for it to unfold after the wedding.'

His comment earns him a withering stare. I don't need to be reminded of the drama that is about to unfold.

He catches the look and nudges me gently, laughing '*Ehen?* It's true now. What would I give to be a fly on the wall when you tell them,' I can tell he's trying to distract me.

'You *sef!*' I punch him gently on the arm with begrudging acceptance of his effort. The smile that grazes my lips is a grateful one. Akin is my best friend in the world, and I wouldn't trade him for anything.

'I'm sorry I laid all this on you…' I start to say, but his response is immediate, and cuts me off.

'Hey. You never need to apologise to me for anything, Karina. You know that. Certainly not something like this. That's what friends are for. It's more important to me that you're fine, and I'll do anything to make sure you're good. Right now, time is of the essence, so let's focus on getting you home, and we can talk later.'

We climb into his car for the short drive back, and he cautiously queries, 'Can I ask you one thing?'

Sigh. 'Yes.'

'Tosan loves you, I know that. My question is do *you* love Tosan? I mean really love him. Because if you do… well, the rest is academic, isn't it?'

I look at him, wondering how well he knows his friend.

'*Does* he love me? I'm not entirely sure, hun.'

I hesitate to mention the scene from Tosan's office several months ago. Akin *would* kill him, best friend or not.

I had found it interesting, in a detached kind of way, that Tosan had been more concerned about Akin finding out about him.

'Karina please, don't tell Akin. He will *kill* me!' He swore that it was his first time and gave some explanation about what I saw. I was the 'light of his life,' and he couldn't live without me, blah blah blah. The picture started sharpening that day.

Feeling betrayed, I told him it was over, but I suppose I let him talk me back around because plans for our wedding were already in full swing. His people had "carried wine" and my people had accepted, which meant that the traditional marriage rites had begun. We had picked out the furnishings for our new home. My wedding dress had been ordered. And all men let you down, sooner or later, right? If I've heard it once, I've heard it a thousand times, so what right did I have to expect any different? Better I understand that before the wedding and avoid nasty surprises later.

So, after much thinking, I told myself I could forgive him that episode and lied to myself I could forget it and we could still be happy together. I didn't tell Akin because I didn't want to ruin their friendship. If anything could, it would be that episode. Akin can't stand people who lie or cheat. When he's given too much change, he insists on returning the excess money, no matter where he is when he finds out. Akin is buff while Tosan is wiry, and as the bigger and stronger of the two, he would have beaten Tosan black and blue.

'Ah, so is that the cause of your misgivings?'

'No. I don't think so. And to be honest, I'm not sure if loving each other is enough anyway. I've come to believe that loving a person isn't enough to build any marriage on so, no, the rest is not academic. I need you on my side, Akin. There's no space right now for you to be everybody's friend. It might all go totally crazy in a few hours, and I need to know that whatever I decide, you'll be on my side!'

Akin does not respond apart from briefly squeezing my hand. I acknowledge him by squeezing back, staring unseeingly, resolutely, out of my window as we drive slowly towards the inevitable.

The ride to my parents' house is silent. I try not to think about how people are going to react, focusing instead on organising my thoughts. I've always been a people-pleaser, regardless of how I feel about stuff. Whether uncomfortable or unhappy, I just keep going until I can bear it no more. I suppose I've reached that place now.

I love the man I'm about to marry about as much as I love my *least* favourite slippers. A part of me has known that for months, and yet I was prepared to walk down the aisle to him because that's the expectation.

Tosan and I became an item in our university days. Many girls made it clear that they found him attractive. Light brown eyes, high cheekbones, square jawline and perfect white teeth against his chocolate skin made him beautiful to look at, but Tosan loved a challenge so he came after me instead. Hurrah for me.

People often say we make a good-looking couple, with a similar look and average height – if you can call my 5'5" against his 5'11" frame average height. My lean body is the result of eating carefully, going to the gym three times a week for two hours a time, and running daily. Tosan goes to the gym regularly too and remains lean and quite fit, but he's not a runner like me and Akin. Sometimes he jokes that I run as if something is chasing me. I never respond, because I think that he just might be right.

'Okay, we're here.' Akin's voice is matter of fact as he switches off the engine and turns to face me, 'Are you ready, Karina?'

We're parked by the ixora hedge in front of my parent's house. There's no space in the compound on account of the other cars and general pre-wedding busyness. I nod my head, swallowing hard and picking at my fingernails. The manicure Preye gave me yesterday is wrecked.

'Shall we go in? You need to talk to your parents, and I need to know that you're fine. Whatever decision you make, it'll be the right one. Postpone, cancel or go ahead. We'll deal with everything else as long as you're good. Okay?'

I nod again, 'Okay.' I get out of the car, square my shoulders, and we go indoors.

CHAPTER FIFTEEN

Karina, 2004

'What do you think would happen if you got hit by a truck?'

'I would die, of course.'

'Maybe. I wonder what death feels like. Would your spirit remain earthbound, or would you go to heaven immediately?'

'What if I go to hell instead?' My conversation with the voice was a familiar one. Often urging me to find an answer to that never ending 'what if', especially when I crossed a bridge.

Desperate, grabbing hands snatched me out of my reverie. 'What are you doing in the middle of the road? See oh! Are you trying to kill yourself?'

The voice that accompanied the firm grab was sharp, and the face looked concerned. They belonged to a girl who looked to be about my age. It was she who pulled me back to safety. A truck trundling by the spot I'd previously been standing in told me how close I was this time. We were just outside the gate of the estate and I was walking home"

I yanked my arm from her grasp, embarrassed to be caught out in this way. I usually could mask these "episodes" – if I told anyone, they would say I was mad or worse. I might be possessed by an evil spirit.

Her voice gentled. 'Are you okay? You looked like you were trying to get run over by that truck!'

'I'm fine, thank you,' my voice didn't sound very thankful, so I tried again. 'Thank you for helping me. My name is Karina.'

She dimpled prettily and introduced herself. 'Ama,' she told me, as she fell into step beside me. We became friends after that, finding things we had in common and prepping for our upcoming JAMB exams.

One day I went over to her house and it was a full house. Her large family and a few friends made it seem like a party, and we had been in the middle of some juicy gossip when Ama was called away for a few minutes.

'Hi,' I started as a male voice interrupted my thoughts. Mildly irritated by the disturbance, I look at the boy who had just plonked himself on the sofa beside me. I noticed him as soon as I'd walked into the living room and there was something about him that caught and held my attention. Maybe I had been staring a little. Or a lot. Either way, it was enough for Ama to start teasing. My irritation eased.

'My name is Tosan,' he offered his hand. 'What's yours?'

I was struck by two things: the quiet confidence and directness of his approach, and the velvety texture of his chocolate skin. I reached out to take the hand he held out, stumbling over my words.

'Hi,' my squeaky voice betrayed my nervousness, so I cleared my throat and tried again, 'my name is Ayebakarinateh, but you can call me Karina.'

'Whoa, that's a mouthful!' he chuckled. 'So, *you're* Karina?' his big smile betrayed a dimple in his left cheek. 'My cousin, Ama, talks about you all the time. Karina this and Karina that. But she never said you were the quiet type. I notice you've hardly said more than two words since you got here.'

I laughed, more self -conscious than I expected I'd be. 'Well, first of all I am not exactly quiet – I've been chatting away with Ama since I got here. And I didn't realise you know who I am. She hasn't mentioned you, and when she invited me to her house to hang out, she didn't tell me there would be so many people here.'

"Would you have come, if she had told you?"

'Probably not,' I confessed.

'Then I'm glad she didn't tell you,' he announced, before offering me a fresh drink. Glancing at my now empty glass, I nodded , and he left to get me a drink, flashing a smile that I knew I would dream of later.

That was the first time I met Tosan - a chance meeting at my friend's house. Three months of mooning about the place, thinking of his cheeky grin, and contagious laugh. His readiness to listen to me talk, his tendency to seek me out whenever he could just so we could chat – whether it was in a group of friends, a party, at Ama's house or even mine. He was staying with Ama's family while we waited for our JAMB results and he waited to go back to Uni. The earth never smelled sweeter to me than in those months.

Kaine called one day on my way back from my run. She giggled when I told her about his latest antics on our weekly phone call, 'Karina you're different. I swear you're in love with this guy. It's always Tosan, Tosan…' she teased. 'I don't blame you *sha*, if he's as cute as Preye says he is, I would probably be eyeing him myself. And this one he keeps showing up wherever you go, is he stalking you?'

'I don't know *jare*, but I like it,' there was nothing shy about that admission and Kaine screeched with laughter. 'Oh my God, Karina! You had better not kiss him before I meet him oh! Let me make sure you're not kissing a frog. Have you told Dan yet? What did he say?'

Pressing the phone to my ear, I walked up to my bedroom and shut the door so no one could hear me. Opening the windows to let in some fresh air, I responded, 'Of course, I've told him about Tosan. How could I not? If I didn't tell him, Preye would have done it for me. Besides, he'll probably find out when he comes home at Christmas anyway.'

'And? How did he react?' Kaine was impatient.

'*Ehen!* How is he meant to react? Is he my father? Anyway, nothing has happened between me and Tosan. I just like him so there's nothing much to tell.'

'Mhmm,' my mind's eye could picture Kaine, lips pursed, single eyebrow raised. 'Try again. You know your brother is super protective and acts like he's your Dad. He's worse than Uncle Naiye!'

We both laughed and caught up on our weekly gossip before hanging up. Daniel *was* rather protective of me and Preye, and I had caught a sharp note in his voice when I told him I liked Tosan. Dan left for the University in Philadelphia last year and was just completing his first year in Temple University. I missed him sorely, and just like Kaine, we spoke once or twice each week. I still told him everything, even though his "man of the world" act was quite annoying now. As if one year away from home was enough for him to "see finish".

CHAPTER SIXTEEN

'Happy birthday to you, happy birthday to you, happy birthday Karina…'

Preye's voice rudely yanked me out of a Tosan dream, reminding me it was my birthday. One eye cracked open to see her holding a small, perfectly decorated cupcake with a candle.

I drew my blanket over my head, 'Go away Preye, I'm sleeping.'

She tinkled prettily. 'No chance, sleepy head! I woke up early to make you this cake, so you have to eat it before you even have breakfast.'

Pulling my covers back so she could climb in with me, Preye shoved her face grinning into mine,

'*Happy birthday to yoouu*,' which made me giggle helplessly. She sang terribly, but that never stopped her. Each year, she came into my room the same way, and each year I reacted the same way until she made me laugh.

Sitting up, I blew out the candle and gave her a quick kiss, before peering suspiciously at the cake. The pale-yellow frosting didn't give anything away. 'What kind?'

'Taste it and see!'

I sniffed at it. 'I hope it's not a repeat of last year's spinach and chocolate cake.'

'It wasn't that bad!' she protested. 'But no, it's not. It's better.'

With an exaggerated sigh, I crossed myself and said a prayer before biting into the cake. Better to get it out of the way. My eyes shot open as my tastebuds were treated to an explosion of flavour. 'Hmmm… hmm. What is this?'

She giggled, 'Chocolate chilli! Isn't it the best?'

I didn't respond, busy as I was cramming cake into my mouth and licking my fingers. 'Man, that was nice! I hope there's more where that came from.'

'Oh ho! See yourself now. After refusing to eat my cake, now you want more. By the way, you have buttercream on your face.'

We giggled and chatted for a while, curled up together in my bed as we whispered about this and that. Preye was more grown up than I was at her age, and very aware of how pretty she was. It meant that we clashed more and more, but all that was forgotten as we chatted before I got ready for my daily run. Mum was still asleep, so I went on my own.

I returned from my morning run to find an admission letter waiting for me – they had offered me a place to study Interior Design at my first choice - University of Jos.

'Mum! Mum,' I burst into her room, waving the envelope wildly. 'I got in. I got into Unijos!'

'Good morning Karina,' she reminded me of my manners.

'*Serido* mama,' I leaned down and gave her a kiss. She was sitting in front of her dressing table.

'*Tobara*, baby girl? How are you?'

'I'm good thanks, Mum. Look, my JAMB result came in this morning, I passed! I got in to Unijos.'

'Ah, thank God! That's such great news, darling, well done.' Her beaming face said it all as she pulled me into a warm hug. 'That's two things for us to celebrate today. Your birthday and your results! Ah, *Ayeba nua* oh! God, I thank you. My baby is not a baby anymore.'

I let myself be held, luxuriating in her warmth and listening to her give thanks for everything from my exam results to the fact that she was alive to see the day. A tad dramatic, given that she was in the peak of health, but I let that slide and gently disentangled myself from her hug. Her eyes were suspiciously shiny. 'Thank you, Mum. Of course, I haven't been a baby for a long time,' I sassed, 'but I'm certainly not going anywhere in a rush. I'll always be your baby.' I flashed her a cheeky grin.

'Since Dad isn't back from his travels, do you think we could just have a quiet day at home? I'm sure my friends will come round, and we can just have some jollof rice and watch telly…'

'Nonsense!' she interrupted. 'You'll go out with a few friends to celebrate. You're a big girl now and should behave like one, so maybe you and Ama can go to the spa today? Get your nails done and so on? She will have some news of her own, I'm sure. Now that you're going to University, you need to act like a lady instead of a tomboy! I'll call Sarah at the Hammam Spa to book an appointment for you. I'll tell her to pick out some makeup for you too and show you how to put it on.'

That made me laugh. 'Mum! I don't think there'll be time for me to be primping with makeup and long nails. And why do I need makeup? Am I not fine the way I am?'

'Hush your mouth *jare*, every girl needs a little makeup and you're going to wear it. And while we're at it, let me call Ndidi to fix an appointment for you to choose a couple of wigs. You never know when you might need them.'

She pulled out her phone and started dialling and I headed to my room to get dressed for the day before ringing Ama.

'Hello?' Ama's Mum picked up the phone. Oops - I'd rung the landline.

'Good morning Aunty, it's Karina.'

'What? Hello?' She was a small and nervous woman with a big smile and a shrill voice that Ama and I mimicked sometimes. It didn't help that she was a little deaf. I raised my voice a little.

'Aunty, it's Karina. Good morning.'

'Oh Karina,' I could hear her smiling. 'Ehen, why are you shouting? Can't you talk quietly? Good morning, my dear. How are you?'

'I'm fine thank you, Aunty.'

'How's your Mum?'

'She's fine, thank you,' and then I hurried on before she could do the obligatory run through of the list of people who lived in my house. 'Aunty, please can I speak to Ama?'

'How is your Dad?' She carried on as if I hadn't spoken. 'Is he back from his trip to Calabar? Tell your Mum that I'm greeting her oh. Are you calling to speak to Ama?'

'Yes Aunty,' this was how our conversations usually went.

'Of course you are. Hold on let me call her.' I heard her call for the maid to fetch Ama.

Ama's squeal as she came on the phone told me she'd heard from JAMB. 'Oh my God, Karina! I passed! First choice.' She had applied to study Actuarial Science in University of Lagos. 'What about you? What did you get? Did you get Jos?'

I laughed as I replied yes, happy for both of us because all our hard work paid off. 'Ha! You got Jos. You're happy *abi*? I bet Tosan will be even happier than you *sef*. Think of all the things you'll get up to,' she giggled, 'and I know you like him, but you better not say yes the first time he asks you out! Try to play a little hard to get.'

We rang off after giggling for a few more minutes and making plans to meet up later in the day, then I called Kaine and Dan to tell them my news.

The day didn't go as I'd planned. When Ama and Tosan showed up, Mum shooed him away unceremoniously before bundling Ama, Preye and I into the car and sending us off for a morning of "big girl enjoyment". The spa wasn't as bad as I'd imagined and getting our nails done while gossiping about everything was great fun. We had an hour with Sarah, who owned the spa, showing us how to apply makeup to our faces - I was rubbish at it, and watched with no small amount of envy as Ama and Preye got the hang of it quickly. They laughed as I grumped at Preye, 'Hmmm, Preye, you look like you've already done this many times before,' I eyed her, 'I'm telling Mum.'

Preye stuck her tongue out at me before turning to admire herself in the mirror. She wore her hair in long box braids, and with sultry eyes, small breasts and already generous butt like Mum's, she had a body that could stop Lagos traffic.

We were given a few bits of makeup as part of the session, and I selected a compact, eyeliner, mascara and muted lip and eye colours I'd probably never use. When our afternoon came to an end, we said our thanks and piled into the car, homeward bound.

Preye and Ama chattered twenty to the dozen, but at some point I stopped listening, watching instead, the life unfolding outside the window of our air-conditioned car. There were street vendors walking through the slowly moving Lekki traffic, selling all sorts of things from bread and bananas to batteries and CDs. I had become used to the bustling streets of Lagos, with its yellow buses (which had now disappeared from the Island) and crowded streets. I'd even learnt to speak a little Yoruba, although, contrary to my initial belief, not everyone in Lagos spoke the language. Sometimes when I closed my eyes, I still missed our house in Port Harcourt, but each time I went back to visit Kaine and Aunty Emi, the town seemed smaller than I remembered.

As I watched the world go by, I noticed a silver Mitsubishi Pajero slightly ahead of us but in the next lane. My attention fixed on a woman who approached the car and knocked on the window to offer her wares from the tray perched on her head.

'*Fine Aunty, you go buy bread?*'

I watched as the lady wound down her window, took off her sunshades and haggled with the vendor. As they completed their exchange, something about the way the seller held her head looked familiar to me. Curiously, I leaned forward to investigate as she turned away from her customer and towards our car. As she started in our direction, her eyes caught mine and my heart stopped. Please God, no! It couldn't be, but still a gut-wrenching ache started in my belly.

The vendor made her way to the driver's window and knocked, '*Oga. Oga, you go buy bread? I see as the girl dey look me, e be like say she dey hungry. Buy bread,*' she was eager to sell the last of her wares.

Her Yoruba accented English sent a wave of relief over me. I didn't need to look any closer to know that she wasn't *her*. Ebele. Ebele the bitch. I didn't pay any attention as the driver asked if we wanted to buy the bread. My ears didn't hear as Preye got on the phone with someone at home to ask if we had bread. I automatically nodded when I was spoken to, but did not understand how I ended up with the bread from the woman's tray in my lap. I just knew that the door I thought forever shut on my worst memories had been cracked open on a day supposed to be full of celebration. Sitting in the car in the middle of the streets of Lagos, all I could smell was the peculiar pong of onions and body odour. I began to tremble.

'Karina. Karina, what's the matter?' Ama's concerned face came into focus as she shook my arm. 'You look like you're about to faint. What's the matter?'

I mumbled something incoherent, and how I made it through the afternoon until we got home, I'll never know. Somehow, I smiled and nodded my way through the day. More than once, someone commented on how quiet I was, but I couldn't do anything about it.

The moon opened doors that had been shut for years, memories long banished strolled in at will.

The silence screamed around me until I was sure I would go deaf. Ebele's face assaulted my memories until I became physically sick. But worst of all, that gnawing ache grew into a thing that paralysed me in ways I could not begin to explain. It was pervading and all-consuming.

For the next three days, all I could think of was Ebele. Not what she took from me, but what she left behind. Every secret vision of violence; every voice in my head telling me to jump off that bridge; each time I was consumed with a hatred that I couldn't understand; and every time I recoiled from authority because when had they ever helped me? Not to mention when I was reminded in church that I was no good; I was a sinner playing at being accepted. *That* was what she left behind, and no amount of running could get me far enough from the bitch.

CHAPTER SEVENTEEN

Three days was all it took for me to decide enough was enough. After my morning run, I found Mum and told her I needed to talk to her. She was in the garden as usual, talking to a plant. Apparently talking to the plants helps them grow. 'Hello darling, how was your run?' she asked as I approached her.

'It was fine, thank you Mum.'

She looked closely at me. 'Are you okay, Karina? You look a bit edgy. What's the matter?'

I took in a deep breath, wringing my hands and twisting the hem of my t-shirt. 'Yes. No,' I shook my head, 'I mean, I'm not okay Mum, I'm not at all. I need to talk to you.'

She put down the cutter she had in her hand and came toward me, arms stretched out for me to walk into. 'What's the matter, baby girl?'

'Oh, Mum!' The tears had already begun.

'Oh dear. *Oya* come and tell me what's wrong. Don't cry so, Karina, it's okay.'

The harder I tried, the more jumbled my words were. Soon I gave up and just let her cuddle me while I panted for air and cried. 'Lord have mercy! What is so bad that you're crying like this? Eh, Karina?'

But the knot that had been sitting in my chest was slowly breaking down, causing me to cry harder. She changed tack. 'Okay, baby girl,' she crooned in my ear and rocked me from side to side. 'It's okay. You will be fine. I'm here. You're safe.' Over and over, while I let it out.

Gradually, her voice soothed me until I could answer the questions that satisfied her that nothing was broken and no one had died. Then she sat back and waited for me to speak.

'Right, so nothing drastic has happened and you're not hurt. Talk to me, I'm listening.'

After a minute or two, I started, haltingly, to tell my story. My eyes remained resolutely fixed to the floor as I struggled for words to tell her what had happened all those years ago.

'Mum, do you remember Ebele?'

'Ebele from Port Harcourt?' she queried. 'Of course, I do. What about her?'

Deep breath, Karina. 'Do you remember how Mrs Ugochi's daughter accused her of molesting her?'

Sharp inhale. 'Yes, I do,' came the careful response, 'What she did was dreadful. I asked you and Preye if she had done the same to you and you both said no, thank God! Why are you bringing her up?'

'Well… I lied, Mum.'

'Hmm? Lied about what? Karina, what are you saying?' Her voice climbed higher with each word.

You can do this Karina, deep breath. 'Ebele molested me, Mum. She didn't just touch me, she beat me and called me fat and stupid.' My voice was raw and heavy with tears, but I did not cry as I spoke.

'My God! Ha! Wait, please say it's not true. What?!' She grabbed hold of my shoulders, shaking me none too gently, desperate for her ears to be deceiving her.

'I'm sorry, Mum,' I shook my head. 'I wish it was a lie, but…' My voice trailed off as I watched her brace herself for the rest of it.

We sat there for an hour, Mum and me. She wept as I told her everything. About the bitch and why nearly all our female neighbours had hated her so. How she took Preye and me to watch her with men, how she preyed on our friends and turned them against me when I said no. I told her about the knife and how I begged Dan not to tell anybody… about the shame and guilt that followed me around – my constant companions.

My narration was punctuated with Mum intermittently blowing her nose, exclaiming and questioning God - 'Ha! God but why?', 'My God, how could this happen?', 'Jesus!'. Like she was expecting an apology from God himself for not watching over her family. Like Ebele happened to her, rather than me.

We moved upstairs to sit in her bedroom and finish talking as she tried to make sense of it all. She had a lot of questions and when I had answered them all; she asked some more. 'When did this all start? How long did it go on for? Are you sure she didn't touch Preye too? Can you describe what she did? Why didn't you tell us? Why didn't you tell *me*? How could you keep this to yourself, Karina?'

Her devastation was raw and painful to witness, yet I could not look away. My emotions ran riot. Shame for being part of something so dirty. Guilty for making her cry. Relieved that I no longer had to carry this secret around with me.

Mum blamed herself, that was clear. Dad would be murderous when we told him later, I knew. That day, she cried as she held me and prayed for me. She asked God to forgive her for failing me, then asked Him to heal and rebuild me. She told me it wasn't my fault countless times. Finally, she said I should shower and change my clothes to get freshened for the day ahead of me.

Pleased that Preye was at school, I did as I was bid, conscious as I finished my shower that there was a lightness in my spirit that I hadn't known was missing.

I looked at my puffy-eyed reflection in the mirror and hoped that telling Dad would be a little bit easier.

CHAPTER EIGHTEEN

Tamara, 2004

When I held Karina in my arms for the first time, I vowed to protect her with everything in me. Thirteen hours of hard labour instantly forgotten as I looked down at her tiny, suckling frame. When it was time to name her, I chose a name as a prayer for her. Ayebakarinateh. A wish that her life would be better than mine. Unmarked by the things that had tainted my days. I failed.

I had been careful to stay close to home when my children were young, hiring female only domestic staff, making sure I talked to them as much as possible… Why wasn't that enough?

I learned early in life that I was responsible for my own choices and my happiness. Although treasured by our parents, my sister, Emi, and I knew that as girls, we were expected to be domesticated and marry well. I always wanted more for myself and was a precocious child. I was twelve when our father died, and our mother simply seemed to give up on life. She couldn't cope and so she sent us to live with relatives in Borokiri, whose main form of amusement seemed to be mistreating and making us jump. One day as I watched my sister struggle to hold her tears in check while taking another beating from our aunt, I decided I would take care of her and we would make our own way in life. At sixteen, I dropped out of school and got a cleaning job in the local bakery, saving every penny I could so we could move into a place of our own. A year later, I put down a deposit on a small room I found near Aggrey Road, away from our tormentors, but close enough that Emi's could still go to school. I taught Emi to make puff puff, so that we could make a bit more money by selling them after school. It was hard going most of the time, but we had one another, and we were at peace.

When at twenty I met Nkem and fell in love, I thought I had hit the jackpot and all our troubles were over. He was an electronics trader with a stall in Town Market, and it wasn't long before I fell pregnant with his child and moved into his two-roomed upstairs flat. One room served as the parlour during the day, and Emi's room at night. The other room was our bedroom, and we shared the downstairs kitchen with his older brother's family. His people said they would marry me, but as Emi and I had no parents and I told them we had no family, there was no one for them to "carry wine" to. That didn't matter to me. I was home and safe as long as I had Nkem. We made plans for our future and I continued to make baked good to sell outside my day job, so that I could still pay for Emi's schooling. Soon, my body began to swell with child, and as I luxuriated in the feeling of new life, I noticed that Nkem paid less and less attention to me.

When I was nearly five and a half months pregnant, I came in from the market one day to a sight that set my heart in my mouth. Emi was sitting in the parlour, on the floor. Her face was wet with tears, her eyes broken. Her face was the saddest thing I'd ever seen, and time stopped for me as I took in her dishevelled appearance, messy hair and the rip in her dress that wasn't there yesterday. My Emi. She didn't need to tell me that something terrible had happened.

'Sister, I'm sorry. I'm sorry.' She wailed over and over as I dropped my bags in the middle of the room and gathered her in my arms.

'Ehn!? Jesus! What happened, Emi? Who did this to you?'

'Brother Nnamdi. He came and asked me to get him something from the room,' she struggled and failed to gain control of her voice. 'I went, and he followed me and forced himself on me! Sister, I begged him to stop, but he refused. He said someone must teach a small girl like me. He called himself my teacher.'

I was numb. What could I say?

'Don't worry Emi,' I tried to comfort her, 'when Nkem comes home we will talk to him. The family elders will hear this. Don't cry.'

After a while, I convinced her to get up and bathe. I took her dress and the bloodstained bedsheet to the bathroom and soaked them in water, to be washed later. All I could think was how I wasn't there to protect her from that diseased ram, God punish him!

I cooked goat meat peppersoup for her, which she could only take a little of. She had no appetite, and no wonder. After she'd had a few sips, we lay down together and talked of our parents and when times were good. Nkem would know what to do, I promised her. After some time, Emi drifted off to sleep, her slight frame shuddering from time to time with the after effects of sobbing so hard. Like a child. I wiped the tears that now flowed freely as I watched her sleep and my heart broke for her, and whispered to myself, 'yes, Nkem will know what to do.'

Nkem didn't know what to do. He looked lost when he came in and I told him. Then he asked me what she had been wearing, as if it was her fault. 'What do you mean by that question? Ehn, Nkem? What has what she was wearing got to do with what your brother did to her?'

'Shh, don't be too loud Tamara. I'm just saying that maybe it wasn't how you think. I've been telling you since that I don't like that short skirt she wears around the house sometimes, shaking her backside up and down the place, and teasing men. It could be that she wanted to do it, but then didn't like it and made up that story…'

I had heard enough. I flew at him in a rage, unleashing the pain of every injustice and feeling of impotence we had ever suffered in that moment. 'Nkem, God punish you! God punish you and your whole family. Let Nnamdi's penis shrivel up and die. He will never be able to use it again.' I rained curses on the lot of them. 'How dare you say that? Instead of you to be a man and confront your brother? *Ehn*? Is this what you're saying? Is it?'

Nkem tried to keep me quiet by putting his hand over my mouth, 'Shhh woman, stop shouting!

Do you want to bring the whole compound here? *Oya* stop. Stop!'

But I bit his hand and continued to scratch, kick and tear at him, tears streaming down my face. We were in the living room – I had put Emi to sleep in our bed while I waited for Nkem's return.

'I won't stop. So if, God forbid, one day something happens to our daughter, this is how you will blame her? You're saying that my sister wanted to lie with your useless brother with his big stomach and smelly mouth? Ah! God will never forgive you.'

Nkem grabbed my shoulders and forced me into the single armchair, applying pressure on my thighs with his knee to keep me in place as I rained curses on him and his family.

'Tamara, it's enough. There's no need to rain insults on me and my family. Even if this thing is true, this is not how to behave. You must calm down and I will talk to my brother in the morning.' His voice was firm, and I was finally subdued. 'Can you imagine?' I heard him mutter to himself as he strode towards the door. 'She didn't even offer me food when I came in, before talking about this nonsense.'

He stormed out of the flat, and I sat there and wept. For my sister and the light that had gone out of her eyes; for myself and the fight we'd just had and for the sour taste of disappointment in the man I thought I knew, who turned out to be a wimp.

In the morning, Nkem couldn't look at me or Emi, who hadn't left for school. I sent her out to buy *akara*, then got up and prepared his breakfast, all the while feeling a tightness in my belly. While he ate, I watched him in silence, noticing how his eyes avoided mine. There was a coldness to him that I was starting to recognise, which was now amplified. He got up, put on his shoes and made towards the door, 'I'm going to my stall. I will see you later.'

'Okay. Are you going to talk to your brother before you go?'

He sighed, 'I will talk to him when I come back, Tamara, I'm late now.'

'Hmmm. Okay oh. If you don't talk to him this evening, I will. And I will report this to your family elders too. Don't think that I won't.'

'I said I will talk to him. Just leave it for now and I will speak to him later.' With that, he turned and left.

I sat down heavily on a chair, fuming and tearing at my hair while I tried to pray for guidance.

But most of all, I wept for what had been taken from Emi and me. Hope.

A muffled sound at the door made me jump out of my chair. Furiously dashing away the tears on my cheeks, I grabbed a rag and started busily clearing the breakfast dishes off the table.

'Sister, are you crying? What happened?' Emi was staring at me from the door.

'Emi... I didn't hear you come in.'

'I know you didn't. Are you crying because of Brother Nkem?'

I looked at her sharply. What do you mean?

'I heard you people quarrelling last night because of me. This morning your face was sad, and he did not answer my greeting. Is it because of what happened yesterday?'

I sighed. 'We are not fighting Emi, I am just angry about what happened to you. And so is Nkem.' I added the last part rather belatedly.

'Sister, I'm not a child. I know what I heard, and I swear to God I did not encourage Brother Nnamdi. I didn't know my skirt was causing trouble, but I swear on our parents' graves I didn't want any of it to happen. And when I shouted, he didn't stop. He said all big girls have to do it.'

She began to sob and I took her in my arms. 'don't cry Emi, it's enough. Nkem will deal with it when he comes back. As for today, you will get ready and go to school. Exams are coming up in a few weeks and you must be ready. *Oya* eat some *akara* before you go to school.'

I took the bag of *akara* which she still held in her fist and put some in a plate. While she got dressed for school, I prepared some *akamu* for her to eat with her *akara* and called out to her.

'Emi, come and eat.'

She appeared in the doorway and edged past the table towards the door, 'No thank you sister I don't think I'm going to eat this morning. I'm not hungry. Maybe when I come back?' She picked up her bag and made to leave.

'No matter how small, please have something. What about some tea? I've just made you some.'

'No thank you. My tummy is not settled – I'll get something in school if I'm hungry.'

'Okay then, wait for me. I'll walk with you to the road, let me buy some tomatoes and onions to make lunch.' Before she could say no, I pushed my feet into some slippers and walked out with her, praying that we wouldn't encounter the goat on our way out. I winced, feeling an ache in my belly on my way back. 'Don't worry my child, I rubbed my tummy protectively, everything will be okay.' But I wasn't sure.

'Tamara,' Amaka's cheerful voice penetrated my thoughts as I entered the compound. She was hanging her washing to dry. 'Good morning, Tamara. How are you today?'

Amaka was married to the he-goat and was perpetually cheerful, even when there was nothing to be cheerful about. Even though I didn't blame her for his actions, how could I talk to her as if nothing was wrong? I mumbled 'fine' under my breath and walked on by in a hurry, ignoring the perplexed look on her face.

I busied myself cleaning the flat and then cleaning it again. I cooked Emi's favourite meal and watched the road for her return. I washed dirty clothes, swept and dusted again, until the place shone. I took out our folded clothes and re-folded them. My mind would not sit still, and neither would my body. Keeping busy was the only way I could stop myself from marching downstairs and scratching Nnamdi's eyes out for what he had done to my sister.

When Emi came home, I pampered her as best I could, finally getting her to eat something. She was quiet. Withdrawn. Her eyes darted to the wall clock often, taking on an increasingly panicked look as seven o'clock approached. Nkem was usually home by six and we expected him home any minute now.

CHAPTER NINETEEN

'Sister, please. I'm begging you not to quarrel with Brother Nkem over this. And I don't want anybody to talk to Brother Nnamdi about it either. I don't want any trouble.' Her voice was low and strained.

I regarded her. 'I am not quarrelling with him, Emi. What Nnamdi did was wrong! How can you say nobody should talk to him? He must answer to someone, and me, I'm not keeping quiet. We are not slaves. We didn't come here begging or for that animal to do this to you or for anybody to mess with our lives.' It was always the same with Emi – vocal, except when it concerned her. The sound of someone at the door sent her scurrying to the bedroom. I opened the door. It was Nkem, his face set like stone. He didn't meet my eyes but grunted in response to my greeting.

I stepped back and opened the door a bit wider. He looked tired and weighed down. Ordinarily, I would take the small, leather bag he usually carried to and from work from his hand. I would set it down or call Emi to put it away in the bedroom while I got him a drink of water and some food to eat. Out of habit, he handed me the bag, and out of habit I took it.

'How was work?'

'Fine. Where is Emi?'

'She's in the room. Why?' Perhaps he had some news, I thought, but his next words dispelled that hope instantly.

'Nothing. I'm just asking.' He sat down heavily and started removing his shoes.

I tried not to kiss my teeth. 'Are you ready to eat?'

'No, I won't eat tonight. Thank you. I ate at mama's place before coming.'

Okay. So, maybe he did have news. 'You went to see mama?' I couldn't keep the note of hope from my voice.

'Yes.' He ran his hand over his face. 'Tamara, this thing you said yesterday is not a small thing. Did you think I would just go and talk to my elder brother like that?' He put air quotes around "talk". 'Your sister's accusation is an abomination. We will go to the family elders. I am a small boy where Nnamdi is concerned and I cannot just open my mouth and be talking without proof. Mama wants to see us in the morning. She will call my uncles and they will decide if your sister is lying.'

I frowned. 'Wait, what? I don't understand. Your uncles will decide if she's lying or not? How? Will they look into her privates part to check? Or consult a *dibia*? Will they check Nnamdi's manhood to see whether it was used on my sister?' My voice was steadily climbing, despite my best efforts to keep it down.

'Shhh, don't shout now. You want everybody to hear you?'

'Brother, good evening. Welcome.' My head whipped round at the sound of Emi's voice. I had forgotten about her in the next room.

'Ehen. Good evening. How are you?'

'I'm fine,' she answered, but the wetness of her eyes told a different story. She got on her knees, her hands together in supplication.

'Brother Nkem, please. I just want to tell you what happened, even though you haven't asked me. When I came from school yesterday, I changed my clothes and was about to go down when I saw your brother at the door. He said he wanted to collect something from inside, so I let him in. Then he sat down and asked for water. Aunty Amaka had gone to the market, he said, and he was waiting for her to come back. Then he asked me to look in the room for a key, and when I went he followed me and forced me.' She paused to catch her breath. 'If you don't believe me, how will anyone else believe me in your family? They will call me and my sister troublemakers...'

'Hmm. It's enough Emi, stop crying,' his voice was gruff. 'I am not saying you're lying. Just that this is a heavy thing to say. Get up and wash your face. It's okay.'

And with that, he got up himself and went in to freshen up, patting her awkwardly on the shoulder. When he left again fifteen minutes later, he didn't say where he was going and he still couldn't look me in the face.

By the following morning, I had decided that we weren't going to see any family elders. If Nkem's attitude was anything to go by, the family meeting would be an ambush, and there was no way I could put my sister through that. Emi looked like she could vomit, and I felt numb from her pain and Nkem's reaction. I left early and went to mama's house alone.

'Mama, good morning.'

'*Ehen, my pikin*. Good morning. *You came alone*?' She embraced me with her elbows between us.

'Yes, ma. I came alone.'

'Mmm. *Oya enter house*. How is your body?'

'I'm fine thank you ma,' I said, perching myself on the edge of the seat she offered. Her hands were clasped loosely in her lap, and she looked at me expectantly. She knew why I was there.

'Mama,' I began hesitantly, 'something happened a few days ago in the house. I know Nkem came to tell you and we are due for a family meeting later this morning, but I wanted to talk to you first.'

'No problem, my child. True, Nkem has told me something, but I want the family to hear it too from her mouth. You know there is a way elders will look at the mouth of a child to know if they are telling the truth. When a person eats palm oil, there is usually a stain on the lips. If she is telling the truth, she will not be afraid to say it to Nnamdi's face, and answer our questions.'

'Mama, Brother Nnamdi raped my junior sister. Please don't ask her to come and stand in front of him to explain the details of what he did. She is traumatised. Mama, as a woman, you know how hard that will be for her. Why don't you talk to her instead? You are our mother too!'

'Tamara, if you had a mother you would know the way of things. You and Emi are like my children, so I will tell you. If Nnamdi touched your sister, maybe it's because he thought she was calling him,' she attempted to explain. 'You know men can't always control themselves. Then when you caught her, she started saying she didn't want it. After all, nobody was there - she can claim anything.'

'Mama! No, you didn't just say that.' I shook my head and got on my knees to implore her. 'Mama I'm begging you to treat my sister fairly. If she really is your daughter, you say a thing like this. Please, talk to your son. Nothing he can do will change anything, but he cannot just get away with it.'

'Keep quiet! What do you think will happen here?' Mama rebuked me. 'You want to disgrace our family? Or, do you think Nkem will support you and quarrel with his brother!?' Her laugh was derisive. 'Nnamdi is a real man and has acted like one! Let me tell you, if the elders think she is lying, you and she will be kicked out of my son's house. You want to disgrace this family! It will not happen. If you don't like it, let her live somewhere else.'

I remained on my knees, clutching her feet and begging for some kind of justice for Emi. And I suppose for myself. What would become of me and this baby? What if Emi ended up pregnant from this horror? My mind was whirling. I couldn't stay with Nkem if he didn't support us now. Support me. And yet if he did, wouldn't that be setting him up against his own family?

'My dear,' she said in the way you would call a maggot your dear, 'I think you should leave now. I have nothing else to say. The elders will do what is needed.' And with that, she got up, slapped my clutching fingers off her legs and walked off. I don't know how long I sat on that floor, but slowly I picked up my body and made my way home.

When I got home, Emi was dressed and waiting for me. 'Welcome sister, where did you go? Brother Nkem has left for the shop. He said he will meet us at his mother's place at ten o'clock.' Her rapid delivery and wringing hands betrayed her inner turmoil. Looking at my sister, I knew there was no way I was taking her to that meeting. I also knew that there was no place in this family for me or my baby. We had to leave.

We were gone before Nkem returned from his Mum's. Well, Emi was. I packed our things and installed her at a friend's house to wait until I could fetch her. Then I returned home and waited for Nkem, while thinking about what to do next. We would have to move to a different part of town. And I had to return to school – I didn't know how, with a baby and Emi to look after, but it had to be done. I gathered all my savings, and some of the money Nkem had hidden under the mattress, my mouth dry. I shouldn't steal, but we needed that money to start over. I made sure all his clothes were cleaned and ironed, and the bedsheets changed, anticipating his anger because we hadn't shown up to the family meeting.

I heard Nnamdi's voice downstairs around four o'clock – he sounded drunk. Nkem wasn't far behind, launching into a drunken tirade about how I embarrassed him and his family, and didn't have the decency to show up to the meeting. He went on for some time and then asked what I had to say.

'Nothing,' I sniffed.

'Where is that your sister? *Na wa for you people oh*! You just want to spoil a man's name. My uncles just insulted me today! When they told me to marry an Igbo woman like me, I didn't listen. Now see what you have caused me. When your sister comes from wherever she went to, tell her she has to leave my house.'

'Nkem, your brother was at fault. If Emi leaves, I leave too.'

'*Ehen*? Carry your bad luck and go, you and that your *ashewo* sister.'

Calling my sister a whore was the last straw for me. My hard-won self-control deserted me and I flew at him, scratching, hitting and kicking him wherever I could. He recoiled in shock before hitting back, yelling intelligibly as his closed fists took out his confusion and frustration on my face and body. I don't remember much except ending up on the floor in the foetal position, trying and failing to protect my stomach as he kicked the baby from my stomach. He stumbled to the bedroom and into bed, cursing and swearing at me until a loud snore announced that he had fallen asleep.

As soon as I could, I dragged my aching body up and walked gingerly to the bathroom to wash my face and watch, broken as the life in my stomach dripped away into the toilet. Perhaps it was better this way. Nothing left to tether me to this family. By some miracle, my face wasn't all that swollen, but that would probably come later. I tidied up my appearance, moving quietly I let myself out of the flat with my handbag and his money. He didn't need it anymore. I had made sure he would never awaken from that sleep. Doing my best to ignore the pain in my stomach, I paused only to spit on Nnamdi, who was sitting down in front of the compound with some other men. I did his wife a favour and told her that her husband was a child molesting he-goat.

'You deranged whore! Will you get out of here?' He grabbed my arm roughly and shoved me.

I gathered myself and delivered my parting shot. 'May that thing between your legs shrivel up and die, you bastard!'

I didn't stop to take in the look of horror on his face as he crossed his wrists down low to protect his most prized possession. Before he could start calling on Nkem, I turned and left, conscious of the blood that had soaked my pad and was now dripping down my legs.

I was defeated this time, but as I made my way slowly, painfully down the street, I swore never to tell anyone, and to protect my family with everything I had.

CHAPTER TWENTY

Tosan, 2004

Life in Uni with Karina was exciting. We met up every day – snatching time together between registration queues and lectures, grabbing a bite to eat at the so called "Bus Park" which really was nothing of the sort. It was just a large space by the school gates where women set up stalls and stools under a canopy of leaves – the stalls for selling cold drinks to refresh parched students, weary from a day in the draining noon day sun and lectures, and the stools for sitting on while they fried their delicious buns and puff puff, often topped with a sprinkling of sugar. The space should have been used for the University's buses, but there was only one broken-down bus there. We jokingly called the park "Buns Park".

There, Karina and I would sit and laugh and chat, forgetting the world and anything else that mattered in that time. It was fun to tease and comment on passers-by, and more than once we caught the women of Buns Park smiling indulgently as they watched us. My friends teased me incessantly and called me a "woman wrapper", but I didn't care. This girl captivated me.

Her almond-shaped eyes were so dark, they seemed almost black, drawing me in. Karina wasn't stunning, but I couldn't take my eyes off her. I wasn't sure she felt the same way I did, although I suspected it. Why else would she spend so much time with me when there were other guys circling, wanting her attention? Did she know that I wasn't as cool as I pretended to be? That I was just "forming big boy", as Ama called it?

'Tosan, if you like Karina so much, why don't you tell her?' During one of our phone calls, Ama chastised me for beating around the bush. 'Why are you still posing? After you won't let me rest with Karina this, Karina that.'

'I'm not posing, Ama. I just don't want to show my hand. What if she doesn't like me back? There are other guys chasing her hard! And she tells me about them as if I'm her friend, instead of a guy who's interested in her.'

'Hmmm.'

Ama's response didn't give me any hope, although I was certain she knew more than she let on. 'But wait, what if she only sees me as a friend? Ama, please talk to her for me, would you? Let me know if I'm wasting my time here.'

'Hmmm. You guys should continue fooling yourselves. I will be here looking.' I could imagine her rolling her eyes and picking at her nails. We changed the topic and caught up on other things before moving on.

To me, Karina seemed altogether confident and mature, whereas I felt like a little boy playing a part. She was intelligent and funny, and her laugh made me laugh, but there was something about her that she seemed to hold back. An aloofness that confused the hell out of me. As the semester unfolded and we both got busier with our studies, it was increasingly difficult to spend time together like we used to. I missed the days when it was just us.

We didn't talk about feelings, so how could she know how jealous I was when she laughed up at other guys? Or that sometimes when she walked by, my eyes could but follow her across the room, opening myself repeatedly to the merciless teasing of my friends?

I introduced her to my friend Akin and they immediately got on like a house on fire. Soon the three of us we're hanging out regularly. One day after I'd endured another round of fierce teasing from the guys, Akin gave me a push.

'Guy, how about you ask her out? *Your mumu done do*. Instead of moping around the place, watching her like a puppy, just ask her out. What's the worst that'll happen? She will say no? At least you will know one way or other.' He looked away as he said the last bit. I knew he liked her, but most guys did.

And so it was that one day after lectures, I offered to walk her back to her place as there were no taxis because of the fuel scarcity in town. Nothing new there, but the apartment where she lived was at least an hour's walk away, near the centre of town. She looked down, considering her shorts and sandals. 'Erm… I'm not sure how far I can walk in these sandals, Tosan. My feet will hurt a bit.'

'Well, why don't we stop along the way and buy some rubber slippers if you struggle?'

'Makes sense. *Oya* let's go.'

The air was humid, but soon a gentle breeze picked up, cooling us and making the walk a bit more bearable. We walked and talked about anything and everything, stopping after about half an hour to buy her some slippers. I watched as she haggled with the vendor at her tattered little stand, which was no more than a table covered with slippers, both rubber and leather, and a tattered umbrella strapped to a stick which protruded from behind the table.

'*Yarinya, ina kwana?*' The seller said in greeting to us. The smile on her wizened face belied the hobble in her step and stoop in her back.

'*Lafiya Mama. Sannu,*' She attempted to converse in her broken Hausa, which made the old woman giggle. Then pointing to the one that caught her eye, '*Nawa ne wannan*? How much is this?'

'This one? *Naira ɗari biyu.*' Two hundred naira. It wasn't much, but Karina haggled anyway. That's just the way we did things.

'*Haba*, will you take one fifty?' and the woman looked confused. Karina repeated in Hausa, '*Naira ɗari hamsin*?'

She nodded her head and spoke some more in Hausa, words which Karina laughed at but didn't understand, I was sure. Money and goods were exchanged and we continued on our way, Karina having swapped her footwear.

'Are you hungry?' She asked when there was a lull in conversation.

'I could eat.'

'Let's buy a cold drink and a snack from that kiosk over there,' she pointed to a kiosk that had a bench in front. 'We can sit down for a while. My dogs are barking!'

'Okay, but let's see if we can get a taxi afterwards. Looks like they're moving again.' I'd noticed there were a few taxis going past. They were full, but maybe in another half hour, we might find one with enough space for us both.

I had just paid for our purchases when Karina shouted my name. 'Tosan, Tosan come quick. I've found a taxi!' She'd hailed a taxi that was empty.

'Drop. Terminus,' I said, giving him our destination and indicating I would pay him more for the ride if he didn't pick up any more passengers, and he set off, talking about the difficulties he'd had all day, trying to fill his tank. I listened to him with one eye on Karina, who had fallen silent.

'Tosan, how are you going to get home? You live in the opposite direction.' She was right. I lived in Naraguta, meaning I had to go past campus to get home. 'Maybe you'd better ask the driver to wait and take you back.'

I hesitated, 'I was hoping I could come in for a bit…'

'Really? You can come if you want, but I'm just concerned that you will struggle to get home. Unless you're coming for Zainab?'

I shook my head. 'I'm not. I don't want this day to end, Karina,' I paused till she looked at me. 'It's been a while since we were able to hang out and I've missed you.' I snagged her fingers with mine, grateful that although she dragged her eyes away, she left her fingers in mine. My breath quickened a little.

I kept the driver waiting as I walked her to her door and at her insistence, stopped there. It wasn't my imagination that she was standing a bit closer than normal. 'Well, I'd better get going.' I leaned down to give her a hug. 'Goodnight Karina.'

'Thanks for today, Tosan.' And reaching for my face, she pressed the softest of kisses on my lips before turning and disappearing into the open door.

I walked on air for the rest of the night. 'Ah, dude, this one you're smiling like a fool so, what happened now? Did she say yes?'

'Nope. I didn't ask her.'

'You didn't ask her, and you're happy like this?'

'Mehn… let's just say I didn't *have* to ask her.' I wiggled my eyebrows to convey my meaning, which was completely lost on Akin, but it didn't matter. She had kissed me, and that was enough.

The following weeks were perfect. We held hands openly, kissed freely, caressed often… but there was one little wrinkle. I wanted to have sex. She didn't.

'I'm just not ready, Tosan", she said, pulling away after yet another session of frustrated passion in my room.

I sighed, growing more frustrated each time. 'Okay then,' I stroked her arm, 'we'll take it slow and go when you're ready.' She didn't respond. 'Any idea how long a man is going to wait? I know you want to… so what's the ish?' Still nothing and her continued silence stoked my frustration.

Time passed. And then some more. Soon it was third semester and inevitably, my friends began to ask questions. 'Boy, have you tapped it yet?' I had not, but I couldn't tell them that, and my frustrations slowly gave rise to me lashing out. Eventually I told Akin and he laughed at me.

'Guy, try and find another way to hold yourself bruh. There are other babes that'll put you out of your misery, man. We only live once!'

He was right, of course. But it was Karina I wanted.

There were rumours of an impending ASUU strike - lecturers were once again dissatisfied with the government. It was inevitable, of course, that the strike would happen. There was just too much unrest and soon we both joined the exodus of students returning to our homes in different parts of the country, where we would remain until lecturers resumed teaching. I did not return to Lagos, but to my parents in Abuja. ASUU strikes usually went on for months on end, and students made plans to travel abroad like it was the summer holidays.

Karina and I spoke, but there was something missing. I was searching; she was evasive. By comparison, this was a short strike, ending after only six weeks, and we were recalled to school with announcements in the leading Newspapers. "LECTURERS END STRIKE, STUDENTS RECALLED!"

Karina called me as soon as she saw the announcement, happy to be going back, chattering twenty to the dozen. At last she could get back to her life, she said. She was leaving a few days early, eager for more than she could tell her family. I promised to join her as soon as possible.

'I'm telling them I have exams as soon as we get back to Uni,' I didn't think she could pull it off, but she did, and her parents let her go, apparently proud of her for being so conscientious. Preparing for exams that would not hold for a while yet. I was excited but cautious. Our relationship promised much but delivered little, and I wasn't sure if we could survive. I mean, I loved her deeply, but her rejections cut deep, and I felt used somehow.

CHAPTER TWENTY-ONE

Karina, 2004

The day was heavy with the threat of the first rains. Grey clouds gathered as I hurried away from the school gates and across the road to hail a passing taxi. 'Apata', I called out. I was deep in thought as I got into the cab. I needed to be out of the house and paying the taxi driver enough money to take me around the Ring road several times was worth the expense, if it cleared my head.

The rumble of thunder called to me as we drove past the gates of Naraguta club, but I could not appreciate it. I love the sweet odour the earth gives off as it embraces the first drops of rain; the hustle and bustle of those caught outside as they dashed here and there to get out of the coming rain; the call of mothers to their children to bring in the washing from the line or just get indoors… but the pleasure of the rain was lost to me. Instead, I stared with unseeing eyes as I recalled the last time Tosan and I had spoken. The anguish in his dark eyes as he confronted me with his awful truth.

Sixty-six days apart. Sixty-six days, four hours and eight minutes since I last saw him. Fifty-two days since I decided that the passion we shared was worth risking my heart for. Forty-eight days since I shyly walked into a chemist and purchased a pack of condoms, so that there would be nothing to hold us back the next time we made love. The first time we would go all the way. Thirty days since I was roughly taken by the youth pastor at church. Five days since I left the thing he had planted in me in a basin beside the doctor's operating bed, broken beyond repair.

'Is it true?' He had flung the words like a dirty rag at me from a distance, as if he couldn't bear to be near me. 'Akin said he heard rumours. You and the pastor from that new church. Karina, did you cheat on me?" His eyes were hard like flint, his pain visibly worn like a shroud.

'No, no, I didn't,' I started earnestly, then I stopped suddenly. How could he possibly want me now? Why on earth would he? How could I explain what had happened after I returned following the ASUU strike? That in sixty days I had changed irrevocably from the girl he knew and wanted. That I carried a secret in my heart that would destroy me and might destroy him too. What if I told him, and he blamed me like the pastor said? Or worse still, if he went looking for my attacker to take his revenge? I knew he owned a gun. He could get into some real trouble.

'No, I didn't cheat on you,' I said simply, sadly.

'So did Akin get it wrong then? You've not been seeing someone else?'

'No, I haven't. Not really…' My voice trailed off.

'What do you mean, not really?' His voice hardened again. 'Let me make this easy. Did you, after rejecting me, sleep with someone else, Karina?'

'Please, Tosan let me explain. It wasn't like that.'

'Then it's true! Oh, my God. How could you do this to me? I've been waiting for you, excited to come back and say I was sorry for being a dick, and would wait until you're ready to have sex. Only for me to hear this!?'

His voice broke at the end. Tosan didn't wait to hear any more. He turned and walked away, and I stood there shattered beyond belief, confused by what had just transpired. I thought he loved me. My visions of confiding in him and him taking me in his arms to comfort me evaporated into thin air. In vain, I willed him to turn around and see me standing there. Instead, I watched him walk out of my life, arms wrapped around my waist as I huddled against the cold and the blazing sun beat steadily down, angry and unforgiving. He didn't look back.

The days that followed were a whole different type of torture. I had thought myself broken before, but watching Tosan walk out of my life made me realise that it was possible for my heart to hurt even more. The weight that left after telling mum about Ebele, returned, heavier than ever.

That day, I went home and sobbed until there were no more tears. Nneka tried to get me to eat, to have a wash, get out of bed - do anything but lie there, listless - but I couldn't. Nothing was appetising enough to tempt me. My heart was as empty as my arms. Dreams of a future with my velvet-skinned babies and big brown eyes lay in ashes around me. I hated the pastor that did this to me; for stealing my dignity and the future I had imagined. I thought of Uncle Akpan telling me that hate was the devil's work. Maybe the devil knew something I didn't, because hate was all I had.

Two weeks later, I got out of bed without being asked. Tosan didn't call and I refused to take any calls from my mum or Ama. Daniel text because Mum told him I wasn't answering my phone, and I said I had malaria. The full-length mirror hanging on the wall revealed a gaunt face and haunted eyes. My eyes flitted downwards, examining my body but skipping over my stomach that I didn't want to look at. Wrapping a towel across my chest, I grabbed my toiletry bag and ventured out of my bedroom.

Zainab was standing outside my bedroom door, hand raised in a fist as if to knock on the door. 'Oh Karina, thank God you're up. How are you today?'

'I'm fine, thanks. Better today. I'm just going to have a shower, I think I smell a bit.' My attempt at humour fell flat as she looked at me with pity.

I averted my gaze. 'Thank you for coming to check, but I'm fine. Let me shower and then get breakfast.' My voice was stronger this time around. I was not a girl anymore, but a woman who would face reality. Tosan might never be mine, and if he couldn't make an effort to hear the truth from me, then maybe he never really was mine to begin with (or so Zainab said). I had told them about the break-up, but not about Pastor Sam's dirty hands or the seed he planted. Shame was my constant companion.

The semester was hard. Tosan and I avoided each other studiously. Friends asked questions. The women shook their heads pityingly when I walked in alone. One or two ventured to ask after Tosan. Like it was any of their business. After a while, I started avoiding the bus park altogether, and found a new place to eat. I avoided anything that reminded me of Tosan. I avoided Pastor Sam by avoiding church and was succeeding until I heard the news that there was to be a campus fellowship and the bastard was to lead it. On the day I found out, I was standing with a group of friends. Hauwa had just joined as we stood in the corridor, waiting to go in for a lecture. She was excited because there was a campus fellowship and she had the job of choosing a few people to form the worship band.

'Well?' The pause was pregnant with expectation as they all looked at me. I hadn't realised that she had stopped speaking and was waiting for me to say something. I'd stopped listening at 'Pastor Sam is coming to lead the campus fellowship.'

'Erm… what are you looking at me for?' I looked from one to the other, perplexed.

Risi piped up. 'Honestly Karina, the way you log out of conversations! Anyway, Zainab has signed us up to be worship leaders in the new fellowship. She was asking when we're all free to rehearse.'

'Signed us up?' I parroted foolishly. 'I don't understand.' Then I realized what they were saying 'Wait, what!? Well you can count me out. I'm not singing in any worship band where Sam is a pastor. Are you mad?'

'Oookaaayy,' her hands were stretched out as if she was trying to placate a wild animal, her eyes steady on mine. 'Okay, it's not by force *fa*. You don't have to sing with us if you don't want to, it's just that you sing so well…' Her voice trailed off and she sighed. 'No *wahala*. If you don't want to join us, no biggie.'

I clutched my books tightly to my chest, seething at no one in particular. The classroom door opened and we filed in. Zainab held me back as the others went past, 'Girl, what happened there? Are you okay? What did Sam do to make you react like that?'

'Nothing,' I mumbled. She opened her mouth to speak again.

'Alright students take your seats. Good afternoon…'

Saved by the bell. I sat and listened without hearing a word of what was being said. Now he would be in my space, and all the excuses I had been giving for not going to church or doing the usual things with Zainab were wearing thin. I realised I was rocking from side to side when Risi stopped me with a hand on my shoulder. Without Tosan to occupy me, it didn't take long before Zainab convinced me to go with her to fellowship, saying Sam was away. Except when we got there, he was there. I sat through a sermon and could have sworn that Pastor Sam was smirking at me, licking his thin lips when he caught my eye. I wondered what people would say if I walked up and spat at him. Perhaps he was emboldened by the fact that I had told no one of our 'encounter'. I saw him often on campus, each time wondering who I offended in heaven for this man to be in my space still.

One day just before the end of the semester, I cut across the Law building on my way to the library. It was late and there were few people around, so I was surprised to hear my name, and even more so when I saw it was Sam calling.

'Fuck off, Sam,' was my response.

'*Ehn*? Is that how you talk?' Whether it surprised him that I swore at him or that I responded at all remains a mystery to me.

'Yes, it is. What do you want?'

'God bless you my dear sister. How are you? I just want to talk to you briefly.'

'God punish you!' I had nothing but hate to give. "God bless you" my foot! 'I have nothing to say to you so please just get away from me,' I turned and walked away.

He followed me. 'Karina wait. Wait! I want to talk to you. I just want to say I'm sorry for what ha … for the thing that… Well, for what I did to you.'

'Please leave me alone Sam. I don't have anything to say to you, because you not only took from me, but you're a bastard. I will always hate you for what you did. I will never forgive. I will never forget.'

I turned to go but he grabbed my hand and pulled me into a corner where nobody could see us, trapping me with his body and roughly moving his octopus hands all over my body while I fought to get away.

'Help me!' I screamed. 'Please help me… Oh my God, this cannot be happening again!' He laughed as I squeaked, hardening as I struggled against his hands. 'It's the devil pushing me, I can't stop.'

'What the hell… My friend get off her! What are you doing!?' It was by chance that Akin was passing by and heard me scream and saw what he saw. Sam didn't get a chance to respond before Akin roughly threw him to the floor and punched him. Once, twice, a third time for good measure while Sam lay cowering on the floor like the coward that he was and begging. Akin would have carried on if I hadn't begged him to stop.

'Akin. Akin stop, you're going to injure him!'

'So, pastor you're the one? You're lucky she stopped me…' His tone was incredulous.

'It was the devil…' Sam whimpered.

'If you come near her again, I will cut your dick off. *No be only devil,*' he picked up his bag and held his hand out to me. 'Karina, are you okay?'

I nodded but was shaken. 'Come, let's get you out of here,' he took my hand and led me away. 'Useless man.' He threw the last bit over his shoulder as we walked away.

He led me to a place where I could compose myself. The Bus Park was nearly empty when we got there, and we selected a kiosk in the corner where the foliage afforded us privacy. As we sipped on the bottles of cold drinks we had ordered, I slowly, haltingly, and without tears, told Akin what had happened. I left nothing out. Not Pastor Sam or the baby or Tosan. When I was done, we sat in silence for a while. What more could be said?

'I'm so sorry, Karina,' Akin's eyes were sad as he looked at me. 'Why didn't you tell Tosan? He would have understood… or at least he would have dealt with the bastard. Instead, he's angry, thinking you didn't love him at all otherwise you wouldn't have turned your back on him.'

'He didn't give me the chance to explain, Akin,' I held my hand up to stop him from saying more. 'And I am getting better. Moving on. If there comes a time when Tosan and I can be friends again, then I'll tell him. But for now, please let me be.'

Akin's hand took hold of mine, giving me comfort. 'Tell him, Karina. I think it will help you both.' He squeezed my fingers gently. 'Meanwhile, I'll be here to talk or listen whenever you need me to.'

PART THREE

CHAPTER TWENTY-TWO

Karina, 2017

My thumb and forefinger absentmindedly twist my engagement ring as I make my way to my parent's bedroom. The ring doesn't hug as closely as I remember. Having looked everywhere else for Mum, I decide to look in their bedroom. I knock on the door and wait to hear the invitation to enter, 'Come in!'. Deep breath, exhale, open the door and enter.

I sit on the cosy sofa that's tucked in the corner of my parents' bedroom with my legs tucked up under me. It's my favourite part of this room, which is decorated in muted neutrals and shades of soft green.

The green leather sofa is old and has worn down till it's nice and supple in a way that only good leather can. There's a cream throw folded on the arm of the sofa for cold days and an exquisite Persian rug in front of it that ties in all the colours of the room. This is Dad's 'chill space' and our 'gossip couch' – the place to congregate when Mum and I have something juicy to discuss, or a secret to tell. Sometimes I just watch Mum getting ready to go out while we ramble about nothing at all. This same sofa is where I told her that Tosan had proposed and wondered at her muted response.

Dad is sitting beside me, holding my left hand as his thumb gently strokes a mindless, circular pattern against my skin. It's meant to be comforting, but I don't like it because it's so forceful, it seems more for his comfort than mine. Mum sits in the armchair opposite me and presses a cup of sweet tea into my hand. She's English like that – a cup of sweet tea for every ill. She looks poised in her black linen kaftan, which is decorated with little multicoloured crystals around the neckline, and her shoulder length hair styled in loose waves down her back.

I don't know how much time has passed since I came into the room.

'Here, baby girl. Drink up. It'll calm your nerves,' she says, patting my hand as though my nerves are the only ones that needs calming. She is obviously distressed and Dad is visibly shaken after what I've just told them. Three cups of tea would be better than one.

I tell them everything, leaving nothing out. I started from the beginning, even though I broke the Ebele news to mum when I was seventeen, and she told dad. Everything started with Ebele. How she ransacked my sanity in her need to satisfy her depraved appetite and opened the door to a world of darkness I couldn't have known existed. How that shaped my need to be accepted. About the voices in my head that reminded me I was worthless and encouraged me to jump each time I crossed a bridge and slowly drove me crazy when I went away to Uni. I speak of the anger and frustration that frequently simmers just beneath the surface after all these years, that prevents me from being really happy. About Sam and the devastating decision I had to make after. About turning to alcohol to numb myself. About my need to look the right way and why I run the way I do.

'Did Tosan know all this? He was in Uni with you, wasn't he?'

I shake my head, 'I did tell him.'

'And? What did he do?' Mum is impatient. She hasn't heard this story before and is clearly angry.

'And nothing, Mum. Let's just say he was "forgiving" and willing to accept damaged goods.' My air quotes don't go unnoticed.

Do they know that their daughter was a nutcase? That I frequently choose silence because sometimes my feeling were too difficult to articulate, and it is frequently easier to play along and act a part than say 'no' or buck the trend? That my drive for perfection was born of a desperate desire just to be enough. Not "good Karina" or "bad Karina", just enough. I talk until there is no more left to say and my voice is raw, but the tears keep flowing. 'Today,' I say, 'I just want to do something for me. To choose me.'

Minutes after I finished, we are still silent, each of us lost in our thoughts. I sip my tea and sigh. Every part of me is exhausted, yet somehow light. It's good that I told them, because whatever happens next, it will be without the burden of the horrible secrets I have carried around with me.

'Don't worry. Don't worry, my child,' Dad repeats for the umpteenth time, 'it will be okay.'

I glance at him. His face is unbearably sad and my heart breaks for him. I remember how he'd reacted after mum had told him those years ago about Ebele molesting me. Dad had come to my room and enveloped me to himself as he apologised over and over again for not being aware of the nastiness that went on under his roof or the impact it had on me. For not protecting me enough. He wore his pain like a cloak, and I am sad to watch him absorb what I have just said. It is understandable that he is fluctuating between anger and heartbreak. I know he'll make sure I'm fine first, then deal with the rest later.

'Cradle to grave,' he often says, 'that's my commitment to you children. To protect you in every way, from your cradle to my grave.'

He will be hard on himself for not being able to keep that promise. Dad always keeps his promises, but what could he have done about this?

'I wish you had told us, Karina. You could have come to me or your Mum. Next to your mother, you kids are the most important thing in my life, and I thought… I had hoped that you could tell me anything, no matter how bad it was. Even if you kill a person, tell me. My job is to protect you. How could you ever have thought otherwise?'

The words catch in his throat. I'm not sure if he's referring to the all the stuff he never knew, or how I feel about getting married. It's almost harder to watch my hero struggle to hold it together than it was to deal with my own problems.

'It doesn't matter now, my love. Let's decide what we're doing now.' Mum lays a comforting hand on his arm, but her words draw my eyes to her.

'Karina, I need to know that I understand you. This is heavy stuff for your wedding day. Good to get it out, but heavy. Are you saying you don't want to get married to Tosan today? Or at all?'

'Mum, I'm saying I don't know if I want to marry him or anyone. Today or at all. I feel as if I'm so screwed up that I don't know if this decision is even mine! Am I marrying him because I love him or because it seems like the thing to do? And am I so used to not rocking the boat that I'm just doing what's expected?'

'Right. I get what you mean, Karina, I do. And I'm sorry you feel that way.' She turns to me and takes my hand in hers. 'Forgive me, but you've not realised just today that you're struggling. Not with the horrific experiences you've had, and not with Tosan. I want us to take time and talk about these things from the past, but that's not for this morning. If you're saying that you don't want to go through with the wedding, well, are you sure that you're not having pre-wedding jitters? Everybody has them. I had questions on the day I married your Dad but look at us all these years later.

Marriage is difficult work, Karina, make no mistake. There are no guarantees that the way you feel today will last. Things will happen to make you doubt your decision, no matter which decision you make. This is not about how you feel or don't feel about Tosan, because that also will change through the years. Your Dad and I have been in and out of love with each other enough times over the years.' She presses my cooling cup of tea into my hand and lifts it to my mouth, reminding me to drink before carrying on. 'But what has held us together is our deep-rooted friendship and the commitment we made to one another and to this marriage. That's what lasts. That's love.'

She strokes my cheek tenderly, still holding my gaze. Her eyes flash fire and love at the same time.

'Oh Mum! What am I going to do?' I sigh and sink to the floor to lay my head in her lap.

'There now, baby girl. That'll do.' Looking across at Dad, she says, 'Naiye, we need to make a decision here.'

A knock at the bedroom door startles us all.

'Who is there?' Dad calls out

'Dad?' My sister's voice is hesitant 'Dad it's Preye. We need to get Karina ready or we'll be late. What's going on? Can I come in?' She tries the door, but it's locked, thank God.

Dad's feet command their way to the door, and he opens it. 'Go fetch your brother. Both of you should come here,' his voice brooks no argument. He's still holding the door open and, as she turns away to do his bidding, adds, 'Be discreet, Preye, and hurry up. Snap family meeting now.'

'Yes, Dad!' Her eyes become saucers. Preye isn't known for her discretion or for having large amounts of emotional intelligence, but even she knows that's something is not right. Snap family meetings are our way of gaining consensus on decisions that affect us all.

Returning to where Mum and I are still sitting, he says to me, 'Get up Karina. Go and wash your face then come, let's talk. There's clearly more for us to unpack, but first we need - as your Mum says - to make a decision about the wedding.'

Gentle hands reach down to pull me to my feet and my Dad hugs me tight, communicating the things he cannot articulate in that squeeze and kissing my temple before letting me go.

I step into their adjoining bathroom, which is decorated in calming blues and greens, and always smells of a comforting combination of my parents' shower gels, bio-oil and Dad's signature cologne, Aramis. Turning on the tap, I splash some cold water on my face and wrists, then firmly pat my face dry with the fluffy, white hand towel that's hanging on the towel ring. I examine my face in the mirror. My eyes are puffy from all the crying I've done this morning. I doubt the best makeup artist could hide it all.

Random trivia crosses my mind: the average human being produces fifteen to thirty gallons of tears a year. Scientists have found that there are additional proteins and hormones released when you cry, which may have relaxing or pain-relieving effects that help regulate the body and help it return to its normal state. So how, after all these years, haven't I cried enough tears to return me to a normal state? Then again, I don't know what normal is.

Shaking myself out of my musings, I head back to the bedroom where everyone waits for me, talking in hushed tones. Preye is sitting on Mum's bed fiddling with her phone, but she stops when she hears me enter. I can bet money on the fact that she's been texting Kaine. My little sister looks unsure, anxious and so beautiful with her hair and makeup done already. She's not going to take the news well, I think.

Daniel is hovering by the bathroom door. He spreads his arms as soon as he spots me and pulls me into a bear hug, his six-foot four-inch figure swallowing mine up completely. The muscles in his arms flex involuntarily into a tighter squeeze. As he draws away, he peers closely into my face and his face tightens a fraction. Before he can say anything, I pull away and offer a small smile. He'll find out soon enough.

'Alright guys, sit down,' Dad claps his hands twice to get our attention. 'You know what we do - we pray, we talk, then we decide as a family.'

The five of us gather around the gossip corner. The tension is palpable.

Dad clears his throat, 'As you all know, your mother and I have raised you to think for yourselves. We have always encouraged you to carefully weigh every decision thoroughly, thinking it through before prayerfully making your own decisions.' He pauses for breath and looks around at each of us before dropping the bombshell 'Karina has told your mum and I that she is unsure about marrying Tosan.'

Preye gasps. My gaze locks on the floor. Her and Daniel's eyes pierce me.

Dad continues resolutely, 'She has told us several things this morning, which I think at the right time you both should hear *if* she chooses to tell you, however right now, the most important thing is that she does not feel like she can or should go ahead with the wedding. The decision is hers to make, and we will support whatever it is, regardless of our personal feelings on the matter. Now, before we do that let us pray and ask God to guide us in making the right decision.'

We bow our heads in prayer, but I don't shut my eyes. It probably doesn't matter much today; God will hear us anyway. With the whole family praying, I suppose he won't be sleeping this time.

'Dear Heavenly Father, you are the one in whom all families are blessed. We come before you today to ask for guidance. Help us to do the right thing, in Jesus' name.'

No sooner have we said our 'amens' than the expected eruption comes from Preye.

'I'm sorry, what did Dad say? I'm not sure my ears are working well today. Is this a joke? It must be some sort of joke, right?' She looks between the three of us – Mum, Dad and I – hoping for a clue to the joke but getting none. I look down at my fingers and count to three. Preye's at the edge of her seat, and I brace myself for the onslaught.

CHAPTER TWENTY-THREE

'You have got to be kidding me! What do you mean you're not sure? Karina? Are you for real? How do you wake up this morning thinking that you're not sure you want to get married? Today of all days. We've been planning this wedding for the last *year*! Why didn't you say before? Like two weeks ago, or three months or whatever, or when we went with Kaine to buy your wedding dress. I don't know, just why didn't you say something before now?'

Preye is about to launch from the edge of her seat, gesticulating wildly to drive home her point.

There are tears in the corners of her eyes. I realise that she's disappointed, but it's more than that. She's hurt, and it has more to do with the decision Dan and I made all those years ago than anything else. But she doesn't even know it. Only that somewhere along the way, she was left out more often, and wasn't part of our whispered conversations, trips to the shops, or even the gist from my calls with Dan anymore. I know it, but it doesn't help me feel any better about her outburst.

'Preye, be quiet, you're not helping,' Daniel rebukes our little sister. His mind is working the puzzle to figure out the reason for my sudden change of heart.

'I know, but truly this is not the day for her to be unsure,' she makes air quotes with her fingers on the last word. 'What about all the effort that has gone into planning? The money that has been spent? People will talk. What about our family? What of Tosan's family? This is embarrassing *abeg.*'

'Enough Preye, be quiet now!' Daniel's voice still isn't loud, but that doesn't stop it from commanding the room. Preye knows he means business now, so she shuts up and sits back in her seat, arms crossed and mumbling under her breath as Daniel explains. 'Karina would not be saying this now if she didn't feel very strongly about it – you know what she's like - so settle down and let's hear what's going on.'

No one else comments on her outburst. My parents don't believe in belabouring a point.

It crosses my mind to tell them about the day I walked in on Tosan with some 'friends' at his office, but I don't. Today is more about my decision and what led me here, not him.

I catch Mum's eye and she gives me a comforting smile. She knows this is going to be tough and in her usual way doesn't try to sugar-coat it or protect me from the truth.

'Alright now settle down,' Dad says, 'Preye your questions are valid, but they're not for now, like Daniel said. People will ask these questions and we will be ready with answers to those who matter, but our responsibility is to your sister. I know that you want to know what's going on right now, but all I can say is that this is Karina's story to tell you. Your sister has her doubts and I'm sure she has talked with your mum about many things and about what to expect before today, however if she's still unsure about going through with it, then I'm minded to call off the wedding. This is not the time to prevaricate. You know that I love Tosan like my own child, but your sister's happiness, her life, her health comes first. I would do the same for any of you. I have listened to her and what she has to say and I know that this was not easy for her to tell us,' he pauses for breath before addressing me briefly. 'My daughter, you will always have my respect for speaking up.'

'Daniel and Preye, I am sure your mother is with me,' Mum nods her agreement and he continues, 'but I want to hear what you have to say if you disagree for any reasons apart from 'what people will say' because that doesn't matter here. There's only one thing that matters. An unhappy marriage can be a nightmare, and that's a life that I'm not willing to sentence Karina or any of you to.' He looks around at all of us, but no one says anything. 'Listen. I will speak to Chief James and his family about this, but my first instinct is that if a child of mine has found the nerve to tell me on the morning of her wedding, the sort of things that Karina has told me today, then I have to listen. She has been through enough – much of which I didn't know of until this morning – and I'll be damned if I'll stand by and let any more hurt come to her when I can avoid it.' He clears his throat. "So, that's what I think. Tamara, have I covered it all or do you want to add anything?'

Mum shakes her head no, but chimes in anyway. 'I agree with your Dad. Make no mistake, this will not be easy, no matter what we agree on. Go ahead with the wedding and you will always wonder if you settled; cancel it and there will be many questions to answer. Whatever the case, the road will be tough but remember that we are all in this together and we will protect you. Like your Dad always says – cradle to grave.'

'Preye, have you got any more to say?'

Preye stares at me briefly before she looks away. Her eyes are bright with unshed tears and she struggles to maintain composure. She fails.

'I already posted on my blog that my sister's wedding is today, and I would provide wedding pictures. Now I will disgrace myself by saying the bride changed her mind. I'm not going to live this down.' Her grumble earns her a death glare from Dad. 'What? I'm just saying it's not just about Karina!'

'I'm mad that clearly there have been secrets in this family when we've been told over and over there are no secrets here. Guess some things never change. It doesn't sound like you want my opinion here, so what's the point?' Preye addresses Mum and Dad, rather than me.

I think, 'Screw this, I'll explain to her later,' but the thoughts have barely finished before my resolve starts to weaken. Perhaps I really am being selfish.

Her voice intrudes sharply, 'I just feel as though Karina has had a lot of time to make this decision, and she should have done so long before today. They've been engaged for long enough and we've been planning this wedding for a whole year, and I know this realisation can't possibly have come upon her this morning. Now you're asking us to support this decision without any real explanation. Is that how we do life?' She shoots a withering look at me now but does not wait for a response. 'Karina, you're my big sister and I love you. The end. I'm not trying to be difficult, but this affects us all and if you had thought about that, maybe you would have said something sooner.' With a huff, she slumps back into her seat, announcing the end of her tirade.

With the look she shoots me, I could be forgiven for doubting that declaration of love.

All eyes swivel to Daniel. He's the only one who has yet to speak, and he takes his time, staring intently at his large hands.

'Karina, I don't know what to say, but I trust you. I'm sorry you're hurting, and I can't help you, but I will support whatever decision you make. Can you answer a couple of questions for me? Because I think Tosan is a good guy and I would hate for this to be for the wrong reasons.'

I nod my head. If he knew the truth about Tosan, he would change his tune pretty quickly. But this moment is about me, so I say nothing again.

'Is there someone else?'

'No'

'Sure?'

My head cocks to one side as I level my eyes at him. 'No. There isn't anyone else Daniel, this is about me.'

Preye rolls her eyes, and I just barely restrain myself from throwing a pillow at her.

It's another moment before Daniel nods his head, 'Okay then, whatever you say, but I think Preye and I deserve an explanation. We will need a cover story, because "She changed her mind" won't cut it with anyone. People will have to be informed, decisions made about what we do next, etc. Uncle Pena arrived very early his morning and has been harassing the women cooking at the back of the house for roasted plantain and fish. He will be happy to eat all that food by himself, I'm sure.'

And right on cue, we hear one of the women shooing someone away, probably with a broom in her hand, '*Oga*, *abeg*, go! How many plantains will you eat this morning? *Person never drink water since you waka come, you just dey disturb.*'

We laugh as the tension of the moment is broken for now.

With no time to lose or talk any further, Dad shoots off directions to Dan and Mum then goes to his study to ring Chief Yeka James and the family elders. Daniel finds Akin and they go together to Tosan's house, while I escape to my bedroom to contemplate what the hell just happened. When I finally look at my mobile phone, two things smack me in the face. There are fifty-seven text and WhatsApp messages from Kaine wanting to know what's up. The most recent one says, 'We're coming over.'

And there's a message from Tosan, 'I can't wait to wake up to you for the rest of our tomorrows. See you at the altar, babe.'

I lock my door and cross the room to sit heavily on my bed before typing out a message to

Kaine. She and Aunty Emi were staying at Eko Hotel, not ten minutes away. Mum has probably called them by now.

I read and reread Tosan's message. Oh God! I'm pretty sure that my bladder and bowels are about to disgrace me. What do I say?

Honestly, I'm fed up with this feeling of heaviness that I'm still carrying. It's probably time to grab myself by the shoulders and give myself a little shake, otherwise I'll never get through the next few hours. I need to confront the last of the truth before anyone else gets in my brain.

Gazing at my reflection, I square my shoulders and steel myself, staring at myself until my eyes are hard and unflinching. Yes, this is the person I need to be to deal with the madness I've unleashed. Obviously, this has been coming for a long time, but if I squeeze my eyes tight and focus, I can recall the exact moment I decided I was not going through with this wedding.

CHAPTER TWENTY-FOUR

The Thompsons, 2017

The soft, firm click of the closing door rouses me from my trance. Naiye pads across the room to join me on the sofa. 'Tamara?' His voice is soft and questioning.

Our eyes meet and cling to one another. The raging emotions within him are evident. His eyes brim with tears and his handsome face has aged in the hour or so since Karina walked into our bedroom. His tall, slender frame – usually standing proud – stoops under the weight of our daughter's pain.

'What did Yeka say?' I don't recognise the flat voice as mine.

'We will need to go over with some members of the family, of course. This is not a telephone conversation. I just told him we need to talk, and I was coming over,' his voice is hoarse and I know he's just about holding it together.

'You should call your sister. Let her come and sit with you.'

I nod but make no attempt to pick up my phone. I have not moved since he left me to make the phone calls and now I wrap my arms around myself, rubbing briskly and wondering why I can't get warm.

'You're shaking. Let me get you a blanket… won't you call Emi?' He points to my phone again.

'And say what?' The warmth of the blanket cocoons me as it settles down around my shoulders, and I burrow into it, exhaling with pleasure. Naiye picks up my phone and rapidly taps out something before gently setting it down beside me.

'There, I've done it for you.'

'Hmmm? Done what?' I'm wading through molasses, my mind stuck in another time and place.

'I've sent Emi a message on WhatsApp. You need someone with you, and I need to go out.' He places his hand on mine, 'Tamara… please look at me.'

I do as I'm bid and focus on his face. 'Yes?'

'Honey,' he applies gentle pressure to my fingers, 'please. Karina needs you… I need you to pull yourself together! Now is the time to support our daughter. Our family. If we are to blame ourselves, we can do that later.'

The urgency of his tone finally penetrates the fog that has settled around my brain. I return the pressure and flash a brief smile, 'Of course,' I say, the pinging of my phone letting me know that a message has come through. I look down and it is a message from Emi. 'I'm on my way,' it reads. I turn to Naiye.

'Look, Emi is on her way now, you go. I'll be fine. We'll all be fine.'

'Okay good,' his brisk attitude is the perfect antidote to tears. He gets to his feet and starts readying himself to go out. Pulling on some socks and shoes, on a fresh shirt, his wristwatch… 'Alright,' he says, 'I'm off now. Wish me luck.'

His feet come to a stop in front of our bedroom door. Placing his hand on the doorknob, he takes a steadying breath. The slump of his broad shoulders betrays the heaviness he's carrying, and I feel so *guilty*.

'Naiye…' I reach out with my voice, in almost a whisper. He doesn't turn around.

'Yes?'

'Do you think God is punishing me for what I did?'

Now he turns to me, eyebrows furrowed, 'what are you talking about?'

'After Nkem…' I clear my throat to dislodge the lump that has taken up residence and try a different tack. 'How could I have spent my life doing my best to protect the kids and Emi from predators and yet fail so spectacularly?' I'm still sitting in the same spot. A sharp pain in my temple warns me that a migraine is on its way.

My husband turns away from the door and walks back to me. He squats so we're at the same level and takes my hands in his. His face is sad, but his voice is firm when he speaks.

'Tamara, listen to me. I too have questions about what's going on here. Why Karina? Why us? I don't know, but I really don't think that God is punishing you or I. That's just not His style. What I do know is this, my love – He won't make a child suffer for something that you did all those years ago and for which you were most probably justified. So no, this is not God's doing. This is life happening around us and we must support her as best we can. Whatever it takes, Tam.' He composes himself before carrying on, 'Karina will be fine. She's a young woman who despite everything is learning to stand up and fight for herself.'

His words quieten my agitated spirit.

'When you told me about what Ebele had done to her, I thought I would go crazy! Not even having her found and locked up by the police was enough for me, but that was probably safest for all concerned. You of all people know how I tortured myself, but I've made my peace with that now. Should we have thought that there may be psychological effects? Yes, and that was one mistake we made. Today is another whopper, but our priority is first making sure Karina is okay, and the second is damage limitation.' He glances at his watch as we hear a knock on the door. 'Thank God. That will be Emi - I really have to go now. Come in, Emi!' Then, planting a kiss on my hand, he releases it and tries to get up, falling sideways and making me smile.

The door opens and Emi bustles into the room and to my side. Ebullient as ever. 'Good afternoon, family! Big Sis, what's going on? Are you okay?'

I give a single nod and offer a brief smile. As Naiye leaves, I turn to my sister.

'Emi, God is punishing me.'

'*Haba!* Punishing you for what? I don't like it when people don't talk straight, Sister. What is going on?' Her voice betrays her anxiety.

I never told Emi about what I did to Nkem all those years ago. I let her believe that Nkem and I had gone our separate ways, and I had lost my baby falling down the stairs. I thought I was protecting her by keeping the truth from her, like I was protecting Karina by not talking about what happened to her. But the reality is, I was protecting myself. Me. Tamara Thompson. A murderer. A weakling. A failure.

'Emi, do you remember Nkem?'

Emi looks puzzled. 'Nkem from nineteen *kiridim*? She clicks her fingers over her head to show how long ago "nineteen *kiridim*" was.

'Yes. Nkem. Nnamdi's brother. The one we lived with for a while…'

'Yes, but what has that got to do with us? With today?'

I take a deep breath and wring my hands. 'Emi… I have something to tell you. I didn't leave Nkem the way I told you. I killed him.'

When I am done telling her my story, she understood why we moved around so much for years until I met Naiye. When I insisted on changing our names, she grumbled, but didn't resist. And when I would not talk about that part of our lives, she accepted it as 'our way'. Except our way had led my daughter to suffer in silence for years.

We weep and talk for a while, just the two of us. When there is a beat or two of silence, Emi fills it quickly, 'Tamara, you know what to do. Go talk to Karina and tell her the truth. Not necessarily every detail, but it might help her to realise that it's okay to fail.'

CHAPTER TWENTY-FIVE

Karina, 2017

Tosan and I were meant to have dinner with my parents one evening and he hadn't shown up. He had text me to say he was running late, and we could start without him. Only he never showed up. I shifted and squirmed in my seat as the pointed glances between their watches and the door gave way to looks of resignation.

'I'm sorry Dad, I don't know what happened to him. He probably got tied up in a meeting and can't get away.'

'Don't worry about it, my dear,' Mum patted my hand, her rings twinkling in the soft lights of the restaurant. 'Let's enjoy our evening. I'm sure he's just forgotten himself. He's probably forgotten to eat as well. Let's have them pack up a plate for him and you can take it when we're done, okay?' I thought she indulged Tosan a bit too much, but kept my mouth shut.

After dinner I went looking for Tosan. By this time, my annoyance at being stood up had given way to concern for him and his wellbeing. What on earth had happened?

My search began at his office because he had said he would work late. It was dark, but the gateman said Tosan was still in the office and I could go right up, which I did. But I was utterly unprepared for the sight that met my eyes. Tosan stood there in all his naked glory with another man and a couple of girls. I recognised the other man from a couple of parties we'd had. I didn't know him very well, but I knew they were colleagues.

My fiancé and the other man were involved in a threesome with one of the girls. Or should I call it a foursome? They were all going at it in positions that would make a contortionist green with envy. The coffee table was littered with pills, the residue of some white powder, and bottles of champagne, wine and beer. Clearly this party had been fuelled by the alcohol and white powder that they must have been snorting up their noses. I couldn't believe my eyes. My fiancé. The man I was going to marry.

'Tosan!'

He looked at me with his eyes unfocused. The drugs gave him too much of a high to react so he kept going while the girls cackled. He turned back to his dirty business without a word or any recognition. The girls didn't seem like they were quite as high as the men and one of them walked up to me and slowly shut the door in my face, a gloating smile on her face.

Horrified, betrayed, confused, and hurt, I turned and ran back downstairs. I've always wondered why people – usually women – run off in the movies when they see something they don't like. I thought it was weak until it happened to me, and I too ran away from the sight and sounds of my dreams shattering. Numbly, I clambered into my car and drove home without concentrating on the drive, determined not to see Tosan ever again and to call off the wedding.

He had come around the following day, head bowed low, looking ashamed of himself. He begged me not to tell Akin. He said it was a one-off. That he needed to unwind from the stresses of work. Another load of bullshit to feed me. Supposedly it was the first time, an experiment borne out of curiosity.

'Karina, please. I'm begging you to forgive me. I swear to God it was the devil that pushed me!'

'Tosan, get up off your knees and get out of here.'

'Ah! I'm dead. Please,' snot and tears mingled, but he still managed to look handsome. 'It won't happen again.'

What happened to the Tosan I fell in love with? Anger is a complicated beast, I've found. How a person can be simultaneously pissed off, hurt, and apathetic is beyond me, yet these adjectives perfectly described me that afternoon.

Somewhat detached, I had recognised the piece of my broken heart, but probably for all the wrong reasons. Images of Tosan thrusting about were mixed in with images of the house of my dreams which I would never happily live in, thanks to his actions. Dreams of finally being able to come and go as I please, no longer having to be home by nine thirty, as if I was a child. The ring on my finger would show everyone that I had arrived and the furniture I had picked out, the trips I'd planned… all these images flashed through my mind as I grieved the loss of the future I had carefully planned.

In the moments that followed, I imagined how shocked our families would be and how they would all blame me because I knew I could never ever tell the truth about what happened. Who would I tell, anyway? Tosan was a good "church boy" who led the Businessmen's Fellowship. Would anyone care? Not to mention the shame this would bring on his family, as he pointed out. Hate had coursed through me because he put that burden on me.

'Why didn't you think of that before you did drugs and screwed other people?' I asked. 'Why do you expect me now to bear the burden of your shame?'

What a coward. I remember he looked so pitiful sitting there in the corner of my parents' living room. I looked for the boy I met when I was sixteen, that provoked flutters in my belly, but he was nowhere to be found in the man that was before me. How did I not see what a pathetic, snivelling coward he was? It made my skin crawl as I realized Tosan expected me to sacrifice myself and my future for him to hide his secret shame. The bastard. I ignored the quiet voice that accused me of playing the victim. Despising him was easier than to take responsibility for my own decisions.

Clearly, I kept his secret. Yet another dark and twisted secret on my back. I so desperately wanted to tell Daniel or my parents, anybody really, but I couldn't. I didn't. Tosan had called me several times every day since then, sending me pleading text messages, promising me the earth, swearing to change, etc. A bouquet of red roses had greeted me each morning since, followed by one or two gifts daily: jewellery, dresses, shoes, handbags... Everyone else thought that he was just excited about the wedding. In fact, Preye had taken to saying quite loudly '*I go love oh*,' each time we had a delivery, but I couldn't summon any enthusiasm for anyone's sake.

Six months of bribery, and each gift felt like another shovel full of sand on my coffin. Naturally, Tosan was emboldened by my continuing silence.

During one visit, I overheard a conversation between him and my Dad.

'Tosan,' he'd said in response to Tosan's greeting, '*My friend, how now*?'

'I'm fine thank you Uncle'

'What are you doing here? No work?'

'Yes Uncle, I just came to see Karina briefly.'

'Welcome, welcome. She's inside. I'm glad to see you guys are patching up whatever quarrel you had recently. I noticed that she was unhappy for a while, but it looks like you're doing your best to make amends.'

Tosan had fidgeted under Dad's famous piercing gaze, 'Yes Uncle. It was my fault sir; it won't happen again.'

Dad held firm with his silent stare, long enough to make Tosan start crapping himself. 'Well, misunderstandings happen. It's between two of you, but if I ever hear that you hurt my daughter, there will be no place for you to hide, son.'

I could have kissed Dad for noticing. Apparently, I hadn't hidden my feelings as well as I'd thought. Now the extra pieces of fruit he had been offering me from his plate each morning were making sense. I smiled to myself before entering the room and putting an end to their conversation.

That brief chat checked Tosan's strut for a few days, but it wasn't enough to take away the excitement of a man being granted a reprieve. That damn strut returned a few days later. When he walked into my parents' home bearing yet another gift bag, Daniel checked him.

'Dude, slow your roll. All these gifts you're bringing to your future wife every day, you do know that you have a lifetime to spoil her right?'

Tosan countered with a cheeky 'Oh well, there's nothing wrong with spoiling her now as well, is there?'

But the day I came out of the house to see a gleaming White Mercedes GLE sitting in the driveway, and Tosan's smug, smiling face, I knew I had made a mistake in keeping silent for so long. Tosan felt like he was home, safe and dry, having bought my silence, while I had slowly suffocated.

Mum often says the only thing you can change in life is how you react to things. Granted, that phrase is usually uttered when she's justifying herself for ignoring the church busybodies whom she doesn't like or want in her space, but still...

'See, sometimes you can't change what is happening around you; the only thing you can change is how you respond to things. I can't stop them from coming to church, but I *can* ignore their existence!'

Contemplating myself in the mirror, I smile tentatively at the girl staring back at me. Full, pink lips smile back at me, a little hesitant at first. I watch her smile grow as an idea takes root in her mind. 'Why not?' I ask her, 'what have we got to lose?'

I'm suddenly giddy with anticipation because I have a plan to escape the oncoming madness of my bombshell news. I'm going to take that gleaming Merc that Tosan gave me as a gift, and drive to Calabar or somewhere no one can find me. It's not running away. It's geographical inexactitude. The phrase makes me smile .

I scramble to my bedside drawer and pull out a notepad and a pen, frantically scribbling a note to my parents to explain what can only be described as a rash decision. I don't want them to worry when they find me gone and I must go before I change my mind. Hurriedly, I change out of my running clothes and kick off my running shoes, noting curiously where they land perfectly perpendicular to one another underneath my dresser , although why that detail is important to me just now, I don't know. Pack first, then shower. My hands grab a few pairs of shorts and jeans from the bottom drawer of the chest, and a few tops from the colour-coordinated row that's hanging neatly in my wardrobe. Almost without looking, each item is thrown into my suitcase. Thankfully, there's no need to fold stuff as I'm flying solo on this trip. Toiletries, underwear and makeup land on top of my clothes, then I jump in the shower.

Kaine will be here shortly and I know she'll try to stop me when she finds out I'm leaving. There's no time to waste. I'm putting on my bra when her booming voice enters the room, preceding her. My kaftan is barely over my head as she bursts into the room, without knocking as always.

'What's this I hear about you not wanting to get married? What's changed? Was it something Tosan did? And why didn't you tell me?'

Her rapid-fire questions trail away as she sees the suitcase on the bed and my non-wedding dress attire, not to mention the caught-in-the-act look on my face. In an instant, she transforms from concern to disbelief.

'Girl, what the hell do you think you're doing?'

CHAPTER TWENTY-SIX

'Sshh,' I say pulling her into the room and shutting the door quietly but resolutely behind her, 'I can explain everything to you, but I can't do it just now, Kaine. I need to get away, and I need to do it now. My hands rise with palms facing outward to halt the barrage of words about to fall out of her mouth.

'The simple truth is that I don't want to get married and it's not *just* because of anything that Tosan has done. It is more to do with me and what I need for myself, which is to not be here. Soon enough I'll deal with the fall out of this decision and, yes, leaving like this is selfish, but if I don't, I'll go mad for certain. Tosan is not the person I thought he was, or even the person people think he is, and to be fair, neither am I. Some things happened a few months ago that made me question him and question myself, and right now I'm not in a position to marry him or anybody else.'

Breathless after the burst of information, my wide smile throws her off.

'What the hell are you smiling at, you crazy girl? See oh! What are you going to tell people? Karina what will you do?'

'I don't know, Kaine, and the truth is I don't really care. But right now oh, today? I don't want to marry. Tosan is all wrong for me and I was going to marry him for the wrong reason: because it was expected of me.'

Kaine's mouth gapes like a codfish as she struggles to comprehend the words pouring from my mouth. There's nothing I can say that will make this easy for her or anyone else and no more guilt will be placed on my shoulders.

'But Karina,' she takes my hand in hers, pulling me down to sit on the bed with her. 'Is that all? You've been in love with Tosan since we were sixteen and I thought we were close enough for you to tell me you'd fallen out of love with him.' I understand her confusion. She thought we'd always been honest with each other.

'What about Ama? What will she say? Have you told her?'

Ama is flying in today from France where she works. She will be so disappointed. I shake my head. I can't think about her now, but I do owe Kaine more than a fob off.

'I know, I know, but isn't the important thing that I'm saying it now? Look, I promise to tell you the whole story later. You're right, there's more to it – I am overwhelmed and emotional about a load of things. You remember I told you what happened in Jos with Pastor Sam?'

'That buffoon! Of course, but what has that got to do with today?'

'Well, what I didn't tell you was that after Tosan and I started talking again, and I explained what had happened, his reaction was not what I expected. I guess I expected him to hug me and say it would be alright… instead of asking what I wore and what I said to encourage Sam.'

'He asked what!?' I expected her outrage.

I put my hands out to placate her. 'Don't make a big deal out of it. I thought they were fair enough questions at the time and of course I didn't do anything to try and "entice" Sam… Well, I explained that at the time to him and he said it was okay. He just made me feel like it was my fault somehow. And he changed. When we finally had sex, it was just awkward. I don't know… I felt guilty. Like I had let him down by somehow 'letting' Sam take my virginity. Is that crazy?'

'Oh God, no! No, it isn't! Oh, why didn't you tell me, Karina? Girl, no wonder you are having second thoughts.' Her sympathetic look made me feel better about telling her. I squeezed her fingers gently.

'I just need to work through these feeling and I need space to do that. Everyone is arriving and questions will be asked, and I just need to go away somewhere for a few days and work through what it means to just do me for a while. Do you understand that?'

'Yes, I get it, but what about Tosan?'

'I'll stop by and talk to him. I owe him that at least. Please Kaine, I know I owe you a better explanation and a full story but right now is not the time. Please just help me get out of here.'

She sighs but swings into action, throwing some more shoes in before zipping up my bag. 'Oya, where you going to go? Have you decided?' A hand pops onto her hip in a moment of indignation. 'And what do you mean by Tosan is not who you thought he was?'

I lean forward and whisper in her ear, as if the walls have ears.

Her mouth falls open in shock. 'That bastard!' She finds her voice quickly. 'I should take a knife and cut off his family jewels! Karina, why didn't you say something? Did you tell Akin or Daniel? No, don't answer that, because if you had, we wouldn't have got here. Someone would have beaten him up a long time ago.'

'Promise me you're not going to tell anyone Kaine,' My phone, iPad and my chargers are launched into my purse. And my passport too, just in case I need it. 'Actually, Tosan did me a favour by helping me see that this won't work. We're in no position to be married to one another.'

Kaine and I stare at each other for a few seconds and I see her struggling to take it all in. 'Right, let me take your suitcase,' she hefts it off the bed, 'I'll take it to the car. Make sure you call me after you've spoken to Tosan. Which car are you taking?'

I smile, 'My new Merc of course. The keys are in my bag and I can return the car to Tosan when I come back.'

'You should keep the car and sell the engagement ring. The bastard deserves whatever he gets or loses, if I say so myself.' She holds her hand out for the car key. 'Give me the keys and I'll get you sorted. No, don't wear your shoes, someone will ask where you're going. Put on the rubber slippers and look casual. I'll take your shoes in my bag and move your car out of the compound.'

'Kaine?' I stop her before she leaves the room. 'I've spent enough time running and I've had enough. I'm going to embrace my fears, my faults and my uncertainties instead. I'm going to confront difficult truths and find the forgiveness I so desperately need.'

'Forgiveness? What have you done that you need forgiveness?'

'Let's just say instead of trying to pray my pain away and continuing to feel ashamed of myself, it's time to confront them a bit more. Why shouldn't I live a little? Or a lot. And what better way to start than by taking off somewhere for a few days? Wedding plans be damned.'

I hug her tightly, relieved that she is standing by as usual to make my life simpler. Preye would kill me if she knows what I'm planning, but there isn't time to worry about her now. Grabbing a book off the bedside table, I sweep out of the room, taking one last glance at the beautiful wedding dress I'm never going to wear.

CHAPTER TWENTY-SEVEN

Dear Diary:

I want to say that Tosan was surprised to hear that I no longer wanted to marry him, that he knelt and begged me to stay with him, but I think he really was relieved.

Daniel and Akin were there with my Dad and Uncles who had gone to break the news to Chief James and his family. The elders were ensconced in the parlour, and as I walked across the hallway and up the stairs to Tosan's quarters, I could hear the heated conversation and cries of "abomination". My Dad's firm voice rang out, 'I'm sorry Yeka, but she's my daughter and this is her choice. I won't force anything on Karina and I don't care whether this is how we do things or not.'

Tosan wasn't surprised to see me. He sat fuming in his room with his group of friends. Daniel stood against the window, arms folded, jaw clenched while he looked out the window. Akin was speaking quietly to Tosan.

Tosan insisted on the boys staying while we talked, so I was limited to saying what I'd told everyone – I simply couldn't marry him, I wanted different things, etc.

Do you think he had the good sense to play along? I mean, I heard the relief in his voice when I didn't mention the thing that happened, and when I apologised, I hoped he would beg me to stay or let me go gracefully, or something. But no.

He went on about how embarrassed his family would be, and the shame he would have to bear being the one who was left at the altar. He called me names that I will not dignify by repeating and while in the throes of cussing me out, ended up letting it slip about the night when I found him out. Without stopping, he called me weak and cheap, and said I had given myself to a sweet-talking man with a bible, and when it hadn't gone the way I planned, I cried foul. That I allowed myself to be bought with trinkets and a car and nice words, when any self-respecting woman would have done something about a cheating fiancé. That cut me deeply, but I had no time to react before

Akin, who had been holding Daniel back, turned around and punched Tosan in the face. I guess it would have been Daniel, but Akin got there first and Daniel ended up trying to restrain Akin before the whole thing descended into chaos. Poor Mrs James ended up running in with the help to break it up, but that's a whole other story.

The bad news is that everyone found out I was taking off. The good news is that Dad gave me his blessing and had Dan and Akin take me to the airport and buy me a ticket to whatever destination I chose. So now I'm in tranquil accommodation in a remote resort near Lake Nakaru in Kenya, and the solitude has been good for my soul. Daniel found and gave me the name of a counsellor whom I could talk to about everything that happened. The month I have spent here is not enough time to unpack my mind, but at least I've made a start and I've rediscovered my faith and it anchors me.

Dan will meet me in Nairobi, from where we will fly to Morocco for a few days. He has a whole itinerary planned and I'm not allowed to question him. I hope we include Tunisia in his plan, but I'm happy to go wherever the ride takes us.

Mum wrote me a letter and she told me some secrets I wish I'd known before. Secrets. Fear. Taboos. She's not the person I thought she was, and she's done some wild stuff, but I'm almost pleased to see my idol has feet of clay. I won't confide her secrets to you, but my goodness, her life and mine would have been so much easier if she had learned (and taught us) to be more open. Hearing all she went through to protect Aunt Emi helped me realise a few things.

I've learned that in order to start with a clean slate, you must confront the dirty. For God to heal you, you have to open your pain to Him in the most brutal way possible. To find your truth, you have to be willing to own up to the lies and be vulnerable. To accept forgiveness, you must forgive yourself too.

My lingering fear was always that if I forgave Ebele (whom I still hope is dead, by the way) or anyone else, it would mean that I would never get justice. But it seems instead that letting go of all that nastiness simply makes me free. So, I'm choosing to be free.

So, Diary, what is the sum of all my learning? That I am imperfect! I am gloriously imperfect! I am beautiful. I am strong. I am imperfect, but I am enough.

EPILOGUE

January 2019

I wake up to a knock on my bedroom door... Well, perhaps more of a bang as my bedroom door flies open, causing me to nearly jump out of my skin. Kaine's voice drives the vestiges of sleep from my eyes.

'Wakey wakey, my lovely!' She jumped on my bed, grinning from ear to ear.

The clock on my bedside table is glowing 7:27am, and I leap out of my bed. I'm late for my morning run.

'Morning Kaine!' I scurry to the bathroom for a wee before getting ready for my run. 'Gosh, I can't believe I slept in. I'm so late.'

'Yes, you are, and you're lucky I'm here to wake you up. Hang on, why are you putting on those clothes?' She points at the leggings and vest I've just pulled on.

'Erm… I'm going for a run.' I shrug and pull my trainers on.

'Not today, you're not! Do you know what day it is today?'

'I do,' I smirk at her. 'Today is the day Akin becomes my husband.' I'm sure the whole hotel can hear our squeals of excitement, but I don't care. He is worth it.

Preye comes bounding in, carrying a chocolate doughnut and coffee. 'Morning! Oh good, you're awake. The hairdresser and makeup lady are here, and Mum says we should hurry.' She stops when she sees my attire, and eyes me.

'Erm, I hope you're not planning to go running this morning, woman.'

'I don't know for her oh,' Kaine passes me a glass of water, 'here, drink up.' They both shush me when I protest.

'Akin will be at the church, Karina.' Preye places the doughnut and coffee on the table beside me, 'Look sis, I brought you something "new". Leave running this morning. Besides, it's bad luck to see the groom before the wedding.'

She's right, we have a lifetime to run together, but I don't believe in luck. I laugh and take a bite of my doughnut. Leaving the girls to chat, I step into my bathroom and marvel at the journey I have been on. And how Akin has been beside me, messy or not. I splash some water on my face before looking in the mirror. The woman who stares back is older and more confident. She smiles a little and whispers to me, 'I am perfectly imperfect. I am wonderfully made. I am powerful. I am strong. I am scared. I am imperfect. And I am enough.'

ACKNOWLEDGMENTS

To everyone who walked this road with me, I'd like to say thank you:
My husband and four gorgeous babies, who gave me countless words of encouragement, sat up with me through some nights and got out of my way when I needed brain space. Above all, you prayed with me, sympathized when I agonised over my characters and gave your unreserved input.

My parents, who demonstrate the meaning of family, believe in me and taught me the meaning of 'Cradle to Grave'.

My fiercely protective and amazing siblings, who have given me a lifetime of laughs!

My tribe and cheerleaders: Kayode, Jo, Kemi, Bukky, Lisa, Oby, Doyin, Rosie and Gbadero… you rock!

God my heavenly Father, for whom I am named, because in you I've learned to fall and stand a hundred times.

Each of you has loved me and brought me to this place and I am grateful for you.

AUTHOR'S NOTE

Thank you so much for reading Karina. I feel like I have been in Karina's head for so long now, it's almost surreal to let her go.

I started this story when I realised that around 70% of African women I encountered and talked with, had been sexually abused either as children or as teenagers. A 2019 poll in Nigeria surmised that that one in every three girls would have experienced at least one form of sexual abuse by the time they reach 25. It's a horrific statistic which is made worse by a culture of burying the dirt instead of facing the truth.

Karina is the story of many girls, and in some cases, boys, for whom shame is a constant companion. The story unfolds over several years, with Karina recognizing what we all must – true healing only comes from choosing life and confronting the dirty. Life is not always clear cut, and we can't always wrap it up prettily and stick a bow on it – sadly, some people do not survive this. They end up committing suicide or becoming abusers themselves.

This is my first book, and I chose a difficult subject to address in the hope that more people will get involved in the conversation and change the narrative. If you